RING
SHOUT

P. DJÈLÍ CLARK

RING
SHOUT

or

HUNTING KU KLUXES

IN THE END TIMES

A Tom Doherty Associates Book
New York

RING SHOUT

Copyright © 2020 by P. Djèlí Clark

Edited by Diana Pho

A Tordotcom Book
Published by Tom Doherty Associates
120 Broadway
New York, NY 10271

www.tor.com

Tor® is a registered trademark of Macmillan Publishing Group, LLC.

The Library of Congress Cataloging-in-Publication Data is available upon request.

ISBN 978-1-250-76702-8 (hardcover)
ISBN 978-1-250-76701-1 (ebook)

Our books may be purchased in bulk for promotional, educational, or business use. Please contact your local bookseller or the Macmillan Corporate and Premium Sales Department at 1-800-221-7945, extension 5442, or by email at MacmillanSpecialMarkets@macmillan.com.

First Edition: October 2020

Printed in the United States of America

RING
SHOUT

Notation 15:

There's a Shout we do 'bout old pharaoh and Moses. The Lord part the Red Sea and all his people run through. Old pharaoh thinking to follow, but when he do them waters fall in on him! So we say, Pharaoh's host got lost, and Shout 'bout all the fussing and crying he musta done to see it. I was a boy when Union soldiers come tell us 'bout the Jubilee. Always imagine them blue uniforms was like the waters falling in on old pharaoh—'cause wicked massa and missus them sure nuff did some wailing and fussing to see us go [laughter].

—Interview with Uncle Will, age 67, transliterated from the Gullah by Emma Kraus (hereafter, EK)

ONE

You ever seen a Klan march?

We don't have them as grand in Macon, like you might see in Atlanta. But there's Klans enough in this city of fifty-odd thousand to put on a fool march when they get to feeling to.

This one on a Tuesday, the Fourth of July, which is today.

There's a bunch parading down Third Street, wearing white robes and pointed hoods. Not a one got their face covered. I hear them first Klans after the Civil War hid behind pillowcases and flour sacks to do their mischief, even blackened up to play like they colored. But this Klan we got in 1922 not concerned with hiding.

All of them—men, women, even little baby Klans—down there grinning like picnic on a Sunday. Got all kinds of fireworks—sparklers, Chinese crackers, sky rockets, and things that sound like cannons. A brass band competing with that racket, though everybody down there I swear clapping on the one and the three. With all the flag-waving and cavorting, you might forget they was monsters.

But I hunt monsters. And I know them when I see them.

"One little Ku Klux deaaaad," a voice hums near my ear. "Two little Kluxes deaaaad, Three little Kluxes, Four little Kluxes, Five little Kluxes deaaaad."

I glance to Sadie crouched beside me, hair pulled into a long brown braid dangling off a shoulder. She got one eye cocked, staring down the sights on her rifle at the crowd below as she finishes her ditty, pretending to pull the trigger.

Click, click, click, click, click!

"Stop that now." I push away the rifle barrel with a beaten-up book. "That thing go off and you liable to make me deaf. Besides, somebody might catch sight of us."

Sadie rolls big brown eyes at me, twisting her lips and lobbing a spitty mess of tobacco onto the rooftop. I grimace. Girl got some disgusting habits.

"I swear Maryse Boudreaux." She slings her rifle across blue overalls too big for her skinny self and puts hands to her hips to give me the full Sadie treatment, looking like some irate yella gal sharecropper. "The way you always worrying. Is you twenty-five or eighty-five? Sometimes I forget. Ain't nobody seeing us way up here but birds."

She gestures out at buildings rising higher than the telegraph lines of downtown Macon. We up on one of the old cotton warehouses off Poplar Street. Way back, this whole area housed cotton coming in from countryside plantations to send down the Ocmulgee by steamboat. That fluffy white soaked in slave sweat and blood what made this city. Nowadays Macon warehouses still hold cotton, but for local factory mills and railroads. Watching these Klans shamble down the street, I'm reminded of bales of white, still soaked in colored folk sweat and blood, moving for the river.

"Not too sure about that," Chef puts in. She sits with her back against the rooftop wall, dark lips curled around the butt of a Chesterfield in a familiar easy smirk. "Back in the war, we always watched for snipers. 'Keep one eye on the mud, one in front, and both up top,' Sergeant used to say. Somebody yell, 'Sniper!' and we scampered quick!" Beneath a narrow mustard-brown army cap her eyes tighten and the smirk wavers. She pulls out the cigarette, exhaling a white stream. "Hated fucking snipers."

"This ain't no war," Sadie retorts. We both look at her funny. "I mean, it ain't *that* kind of war. Nobody down there watching for snipers. Besides, only time you see Winnie is before she put one right between the eyes." She taps her forehead and smiles crookedly, a wad of tobacco bulging one cheek.

Sadie's no sniper. But she ain't lying. Girl can shoot the wings off a fly. Never one day in Uncle Sam's army neither—just hunting with her grandpappy in Alabama. "Winnie" is her Winchester 1895, with a walnut stock, an engraved slate-gray receiver, and a twenty-four-inch barrel. I'm not big on guns, but got to admit—that's one damn pretty killer.

"All this waiting making me fidgety," she huffs, pulling at the red-and-black-checkered shirt under her overalls. "And I can't pass time reading fairy tales like Maryse."

"Folktales." I hold up my book. "Say so right on the cover."

"Whichever. Stories 'bout Bruh Fox and Bruh Bear sound like fairy tales to me."

"Better than those trashy tabloids you like," I retort.

"Been told y'all there's truth in there. Just you watch. Anyway, when we gon' kill something? This taking too long!"

Can't argue there. Been three-quarters of an hour now we out here and this Macon sun ain't playing at midday. My nice plaited and pinned-up hair gone damp beneath my tan newsboy cap. Perspiration sticking my striped white shirt to my back. And these gray wool knickers ain't much better. Prefer a summer dress loose on my hips I can breathe in. Don't know how men stay all confined like this.

Chef stands, dusting off and taking a last savoring drag on the Chesterfield before stamping it beneath a faded Pershing boot. I'm always impressed by her height—taller than me certainly, and some men for that matter. She lean too, all dark long legs and arms fitted into a tan combat tunic and breeches. Imagine the kaiser's men musta choked on their sauerkraut seeing her and the Black Rattlers charging in the Meuse-Argonne.

"In the trenches only thing living besides us was lice and rats. Lice was damn useless. Rats you could eat. Just had to know the proper bait and trap."

Sadie gags like she swallowed her tobacco. "Cordelia Lawrence, of all the nasty stories you done told about that nasty war, that is by far the *nastiest*!"

"Cordy, you ate rats?"

Chef just chuckles before walking off. Sadie looks to me,

mimicking throwing up. I tighten the laces on my green gaiters before standing and stuff my book into a back pocket. When I reach Chef she at the other end of the roof, peering off the edge.

"Like I say," she picks up again. "You want to catch a rat, get the right bait and trap. Then, you just wait him out."

Sadie and I follow her gaze to the alley tucked behind the building, away from the parade and where nobody likely to come. On the ground is our bait. A dog carcass. It's been cut to pieces, the innards spilled out bloody and pink on the paving stones amid charred black fur. The stink of it carries even up here.

"You have to chop it up like that?" I ask, my belly unsettled.

Chef shrugs. "You want to catch bees, you gotta put out enough honey."

Like how Bruh Fox catch Bruh Rabbit, I imagine my brother saying.

"Look like all we catching is flies," Sadie mutters. She leans over the ledge to spit tobacco at the carcass, missing wide.

I cut my eyes to her. "Could you be more respectful?"

Sadie scrunches up her face, chewing harder. "Dog dead. Spit won't hurt it none."

"Still, we can try not to be vulgar."

She snorts. "Carrying on over a dog when we put down worse."

I open my mouth, then decide answering ain't worth the bother.

"Macon not missing another stray," Chef says. "If it helps, ol' girl never saw her end coming." She pats the German trench knife at her waist—her prize souvenir. It don't help. We take to staring at the dog, the hurly-burly of the parade at our backs in our ears.

"I wonder why Ku Kluxes like dog?" Sadie asks, breaking our quiet.

"Seared but bloody," Chef adds. "Roasted that one on a spit."

"That's what I'm saying. Why dog and not, say, chicken? Or hogs?"

"Maybe they ain't got chickens where they from, or hogs—just got dogs."

"Or something that *taste* like dog."

My belly could do without this particular conversation, but when Sadie on a rant, best just ride it out.

"Maybe I shoulda put some pepper and spices on it," Chef jokes.

Sadie waves her off. "White folk don't care 'bout pepper and spices. Like they food bland as water."

Chef squints over her high cheekbones as loud sky rockets go off, followed by the booms of gas bottle bombs. "I dunno. When we was in France, them Frenchies could put they foot on up in some food."

Sadie's eyes narrow. "You talking rats again, Cordy?"

"Not in the trenches. In Paris, where we was after the

armistice. Frenchie gals loved cooking for colored soldiers. Liked doing a heap more than cooking too." She flashes the wink and smile of a rogue. "Had us some steak tartare and cassoulet, duck confit, ratatouille—Sadie, fix your face, ratatouille not made from rats."

Sadie don't look convinced. "Well, don't know what type of white folk they got in France. But the ones here don't put no proper seasoning in they food unless they got Niggers to do so for 'em." Her eyes widen. "I wonder what Niggers smell like to Ku Kluxes? You think Niggers smell like burnt dog to their noses, and that's why they come after us so? I wonder if there's even Niggers where they from? And if—"

"Sadie!" I snap, losing what little patience I got. "Heaven knows I asked you more than once to stop using that word. At least in my presence?"

That yella gal rolls her eyes so hard at me it's a wonder she don't fall asleep. "Why you frettin', Maryse? Always says my Niggers with a big *N*."

I glare at her. "And that make a difference how?"

She has the gall to frown like I'm simple. "Why with a big *N*, it's respectful like."

Seeing me at a loss, Chef intervenes. "And how can we tell if you using a big *N* or a common *n*?"

Now Sadie takes to staring at both of us, like we don't understand two plus two is four. "Why would I use a small *n* nigger? That's insulting!"

I can see Chef's stumped now too. They could get all the

scientists the world over to try and figure out how Sadie's mind works—wouldn't do no good. Chef soldiers on anyway. "So can white folk ever use a big *N* Nigger?"

Sadie shakes her head, as if this is all settled scripture written down between Leviticus and Deuteronomy. "Never! White folk always mean the small *n*! And if they try to say it with the big *N*, you should put they front teeth in the back of they mouth. Honestly, you two! What kind of Niggers even need to ask me that?"

I purse my lips up into their full rounded glory, set to tell her exactly *what kind,* but Chef holds up a fist and we drop to peer over the rooftop wall. There's three Ku Kluxes entering the alley.

They dressed in white robes, with the hoods pulled up. The first one is tall and lanky, with an Adam's apple I can spot from here. His eyes dart around the alley, while a nose like a beak sniffs the air. When he spots the dog carcass he slinks over, still sniffing. The two other Ku Kluxes— one short and portly, the other a broad-chested block of muscle—soon join him.

I can tell right off there's something's peculiar about them. Not just those silly costumes neither. Or because they sniffing at a chopped-up, half-burnt dog like regular folk sniff a meal. They don't walk right—all jerky and stiff. And they breathing too fast. Those things anybody can notice, if they paying attention. But what only a few can see—people like me, Sadie, and Chef—is the way the faces on these men move. And I mean *move.* They don't stay still for nothing—wobbling and twisting about, like reflections in those funny mirrors at carnivals.

The first Ku Klux goes down on all fours, palms flat and back legs bent so he's raised up on his toes. He sticks out a tongue to take a long lick at the dog carcass, smearing his lips and chin bloody. A growl in the back of his throat sends a tickle up my spine. Then with a quickness, he opens his mouth full and plunges teeth-first into the carcass, tearing out and swallowing chunks of dogmeat. The other two scramble over on all fours, all of them feeding at once. It makes my stomach do somersaults.

My eyes flick to Sadie. She already crouched into position, Winnie aimed, eyes fixed, and her breathing steady. There's no more chewing tobacco or any talk. When she ready to shoot, she can be calm as a spring rain.

"Think you can hit it from here?" Chef whispers. "They all so close together!"

Sadie don't answer, gone still as a statue. Then, as a fierce thunder of firecrackers goes off at the parade, she pulls the trigger. That bullet flies right between the open crook of a Ku Klux's bent elbow, hitting the dog carcass, and striking what Chef buried inside.

Back in the war, Cordy picked up the nickname Chef. Not for cooking—at least not food. Frenchie soldiers learned her to make things for blowing up Germans and collapsing trenches—like what she stuffed in that carcass. Soon as Sadie's bullet punches through dog flesh, the whole thing explodes! The blast louder than those bottle bombs, and I duck, covering my ears. When I dare to peek back down, there's nothing left of the dog but a red smear. The Ku Kluxes all laid out. The lanky one got half his face blowed off. Another missing an arm, while the big one's chest look caved in.

"Lord, Cordy!" I gasp. "How big a bomb you put in there?"

She stands there grinning, marveling at her handiwork. "Big enough, I think."

Wasn't just blasting powder that took down the Ku Kluxes. That dog was filled with silver pellets and iron slags. Best way to put down one of these haints. I fish a sidewinder pocket watch from my knickers, glancing at the open-face front.

"You and Sadie bring the truck." I nod at the Ku Kluxes. "I'll get them ready for hauling. Hurry now. We ain't got much time."

"Why I got to go get the truck?" Sadie whines.

"Because we need to get a yella gal with a big ol' gun off the streets," Chef retorts, throwing a rope over the warehouse edge.

I don't wait to argue Sadie's complaints; she got lots of those. Grabbing hold of the rope, I start making my way down. Tried our best to mask what we been doing. But anybody come looking and find three dead Ku Kluxes and three colored women—well, that's for sure trouble.

I'm about halfway to the ground when Sadie calls out, "I think they moving."

"What?" Chef asks, just above me. "Get on down the rope, gal, and let's go—"

Sadie again: "I'm telling y'all, them Ku Kluxes is moving!"

What she going on about now? I twist about on the rope, holding to the thick cord with my legs locked onto the bottom. My heart catches. The Ku Kluxes *are* moving! The big one sitting up, feeling at his caved-in chest. The portly one's stirring too, looking to his missing arm. But it's the lanky one that jumps up first, face half gone so that you can see bone showing. His good eye rolls around till it lands on me and he opens his mouth to let out a screech that ain't no ways human. That's when I know, things about to get bad.

The sickening sound of bone cracking, of muscle and flesh stretching and pulling, fills the alley. The lanky man's body grows impossibly large, tearing out his skin as easy as it shreds away his white robes. The thing standing in his place now can't rightly be called a man. It's easily nine feet tall, with legs that bend back like the hindquarters of a beast, joined to a long torso twice as wide as most men. Arms of thick bone and muscle jut from its shoulders, stretching to the ground. But it's the head that stands out—long and curved to end in a sharp bony point.

This is a Ku Klux. A *real* Ku Klux. Every bit of the thing is a pale bone white, down to claws like carved blades of ivory. The only part not white are the eyes. Should be six in all: beads of red on black in rows of threes on either side of that curving head. But just like the lanky man, half its face been ripped away by Chef's bomb. The eyes that's left are all locked on me now, though. And what passes for lips on a long muzzle peel back, revealing a nest of teeth like spiky icicles—before it lunges.

Watching a Ku Klux raging at me while dangling off the side of a building is one sight I could do with forgetting. There's the crack of a rifle and a bullet takes it in the shoulder. Another crack and a second bullet punches its chest. I glance up to find Sadie, looking like a photo I once seen of Stagecoach Mary, shells flying as she works the lever. She hits the Ku Klux two more times before stopping to reload. That don't kill it, though—just sends it reeling back, bleeding, in pain, and mad as hell.

Still, Sadie's bought me precious seconds. Above, Chef is calling with an arm extended. But I won't make that climb—not before the Ku Klux is on me. Searching frantic for a way out, my eyes land on a window. I slide down the rope, palms burning on the coarse fibers. Please let it be open! Not open, but I almost shout, "Hallelujah!" when I see it's missing glass on one side. I grab the upper edge with a hand while planting a brown Oxford on the bottom. Above I hear shouts, and from the corner of my eye catch the Ku Klux running for me and leaping, claws extended and mouth wide.

I push through that open slot and practically fall inside, just before the Ku Klux hits the wall. A long snout breaks through the remaining glass, snapping at air. Sadie's rifle goes off again, and the monster roars in pain. Turning its gaze up, it digs bony claws into the brick and starts to climb.

I watch all this lying on a bale of cotton. Lucky, because I'd be a sight more tore up landing on the wood floor. Still, that fall hurt something awful. It takes a moment to roll off my back and stumble to my feet, feeling bruised all over. Except for sunlight streaking through windows, it's dark in here. Stifling hot too. I shake my head to clear it. Don't hear no more rifle shots, but I know there must be a fight on the roof. Need to get back up there to help Chef and Sadie. Need to—

Something heavy rams the warehouse doors, making me jump. Did somebody finally hear all the noise we making behind the fireworks and whatnot and come looking? But when the doors get hit again, strong enough to almost buckle them, I know that's not people. Only thing big enough to do that is—the doors are ripped near off their hinges before I can finish the thought, spilling in daylight and monsters. The two other Ku Kluxes. My luck done run out.

They easy enough to recognize. One missing an arm. The other, possibly the biggest Ku Klux I ever seen, got a dent in its pale white chest. The two sniff at the air, searching. Ku Kluxes don't have good eyesight, even though they got six. But they can smell better than the best hound. It takes two heartbeats for them fix on me. Then they're galloping on all fours, snarling and marking me as prey.

But like I said already, I hunt monsters.

And I got a sword that sings.

It comes to me at a thought and a half-whispered prayer,

pulled from nothingness into my waiting grip—a silver hilt joined to smoke that moves like black oil before dripping away. The flat, leaf-shaped blade it leaves behind is almost half my height, with designs cut into the dark iron. Visions dance in my head as they always do when the sword comes: a man pounding out silver with raw, cut-up feet in a mine in Peru; a woman screaming and pushing out birth blood in the bowels of a slave ship; a boy, wading to his chest in a rice field in the Carolinas.

And then there's the girl. Always her. Sitting in a dark place, shaking all over, wide eyes staring up at me with fright. That fear is powerful strong—like a black lake threatening to anoint me in a terrible baptism.

Go away! I whisper. And she do.

Except for the girl, the visions always different. People dead now for Lord knows how long. Their spirits are drawn to the sword, and I can hear them chanting—different tongues mixing into a harmony that washes over me, settling onto my skin. It's them that compel the ones bound to the blade—the chiefs and kings who sold them away—to call on old African gods to rise up, and dance in time to the song.

All this happens in a few blinks. My sword is up and gripped two-fisted to meet the Ku Kluxes bearing down on me. Big as it is, the blade is always the same easy balanced weight—like it was made just for me. In a sudden burst the black iron explodes with light like one of them African gods cracked open a brilliant eye.

The first Ku Klux is blinded by the glare. It stops short, reaching its remaining arm to put out the small star. I dance back, moving to chants thrumming in my head, their rhythm my guide, and swing. The blade cuts flesh and bone like tough meat. The Ku Klux shrieks at losing a second arm. I follow through with a slash at its exposed neck, and the monster crashes down, gurgling on dark spurting blood. The bigger Ku Klux lumbers right atop it to reach me and there's a sharp crack I think is the wounded monster's spine.

One down.

But that big Ku Klux not giving me time to rest. It launches at me, and I jump out the way before I get crushed. I give a good biting slash as I do and it howls, but lunges again, snapping jaws almost catching my arm. I duck, moving deeper into the maze of bundled cotton, zigzagging before squeezing into a space and going still.

I can hear the Ku Klux, raking claws through cotton bales, searching for me. My sword has thankfully gone dark. But I won't stay hidden long. I have to become the hunter again. End this.

C'mon, Bruh Rabbit, my brother urges. Think up a trick to fool ol' Bruh Bear!

Pulling out my pocket watch, I kiss it once. Quick as I can, I rise up and hurl it clattering across the wood floor. The Ku Klux whips about, tearing after the noise. As it does I climb onto the bales, running and hopping from one to the other, until I get to where it's hunched over, sniffing the pocket watch—before smashing it under a clawed foot.

That makes me madder than all else.

With a cry I hurl myself at it, the chants in my head rising to a fever pitch.

I land on the monster's back, the blade sinking through flesh into the base of its neck. Before it can throw me off I clutch at ridges on its pointed head and with my whole body push the blade up and deep. The Ku Klux jerks once before collapsing facedown, like its bones turned to jelly. I fall with it, careful not to get rolled under, still gripping the silver hilt of my sword. Regaining my breath, I do a quick check to make sure nothing's broken. Then, pushing to my feet, I press a boot onto the dead thing's back and pull the blade free. Dark blood sizzles off the black iron like water on a hot skillet.

Catching movement out the corner of my eye I spin about. But it's Chef and Sadie. Relief forces my muscles to relax and the chanting in my head lowers to a murmur. Chef lets out a low whistle seeing the two dead Ku Kluxes. Sadie just grunts—closest she comes to a compliment. I must look a sight. Somewhere along the way I lost my cap, and my undone hair is framing my coffee-brown face in a tangled black cloud.

"Called up your little pig sticker?" Sadie asks, eyeing my sword.

"The one up top?" I ask, ignoring her and breathing hard.

Sadie pats Winnie in answer. "Took a mess of bullets too."

"And this knife when things got close," Chef adds, patting her war souvenir.

Outside the parade's moved on. But I can still hear the brass band and fireworks. As if a whole lot of monster battling ain't happened just some streets over. Still, somebody over there bound to know the difference between firecrackers and a rifle.

"Let's get moving," I say. "Last thing we need is police."

Macon's constables and the Klan not on good terms. Surprising, ain't it? Seems the police don't take well to them threatening to run one of their own for sheriff. That don't mean the police friendly with colored folk, though. So we try not to cross them.

When Bruh Bear and Bruh Lion get to fighting, I remember my brother saying, *Bruh Rabbit best steer clear!*

Chef nods. "C'mon, yella gal—say, what you doing there?"

I turn to find Sadie poking at a cotton bale with her rifle.

"Y'all ain't ever worked a field," she's muttering, "so don't expect you to know better. But July is when the harvest just starting. Warehouse like this should be empty."

"So?" I glance nervous at the alley. Don't got time for this.

"So," she throws back at me, reaching inside a bale. "I want to see what they hiding." Her arm comes back, holding a dark glass bottle. Grinning, she pulls out the cork and takes a swig that sets her shivering.

"Tennessee whiskey!" she hoots.

Chef dives for another bale, digging with her knife to pull out two more bottles.

I give Sadie my own grunt. Tennessee whiskey worth a

pretty penny, what with the Prohibition still on. And this little monster-hunting operation costs money.

"We'll take what we can, but we need to hurry!"

I look down at the dead Ku Klux. The monster's bone-white skin is already turned gray, scraps peeling and floating into the air like ashes of paper, turning to dust before our eyes. That's what happens to a Ku Klux when its killed. Body just crumbles away, as if it don't belong here—which I assure you it *does not*. In about twenty minutes won't be no blood or bones or nothing—just dust. Make it feel like you fighting shadows.

"You need help with—?" Chef gestures at the dead Ku Klux.

I shake my head, hefting my sword. "Y'all bring the truck. Nana Jean been expecting us. I got this."

Sadie huffs. "All that fuss over a dog, and this don't make you blink."

I watch them go before fixing my eyes back to the dead Ku Klux. Sadie should know better. That dog didn't hurt nobody. These haints evil and need putting down. I ain't got a bit of compunction about that. Lifting my sword, I bring it down with a firm swing, severing the Ku Klux's forearm at the elbow. Blood and gore splatters me, turning at once to motes of dust. In my head the chanting of long-dead slaves and bound-up chiefs starts up again. I find myself humming along, lost to the rhythm of my singing blade, as I set about my grisly work.

TWO

The parade dies away as we leave downtown Macon in our beat-up old Packard, with its faded green doors, rattling engine, and patched-up wheels. But it runs good as the newer motor trucks, Chef insists. She at the wheel, filling up the cab with thick oaky cigarette smoke.

"Why come I always got to sit in the middle?" Sadie complains, scrunched tight against us with the Winchester between her knees. "And why Cordy always get to drive?"

"Because I'm oldest," Chef answers around her Chesterfield.

"So? I made twenty-one last month. Six years more don't make much."

"How about this. I'm the one who drove these back in France. And if I can dodge German mines I can avoid Macon's potholes." She swerves as if to prove her point.

"Well, why Maryse get the door? She ain't but four years older than me."

"Because I don't hang out the window trying to shoot rabbits?"

Sadie rolls her eyes. "First you sweet on dogs, now rabbits."

"If you like, could ride in the back." Chef jerks a thumb to the truck's bed covered by a bulging tan canopy. Sadie grumbles and hunches down with a miserable look. Nobody wants to sit with what we hauling.

I take to gazing out the window, reading advertisements plastering the walls of downtown Macon. One is for Wrigley's Spearmint Chewing Gum. There's another with the Uneeda Biscuit boy in his yellow raincoat, carrying a box of crackers. But what my eyes fix on is a poster taking up the whole side of a building. It shows two Civil War soldiers—one in blue, the other gray—shaking hands under a gaudy American flag. *D. W. Griffith presents* is printed in red, then in big white letters, *THE BIRTH OF A NATION*. "Come see the rerelease of the film that thrilled the country!" a caption reads. "Sunday, at Stone Mountain!"

Sadie leans over me, stretching out the window to hurl curses at the poster.

Can't say I blame her.

You see, the Second Klan was birthed on November 25 back in 1915. What we call D-Day, or Devil's Night—when William Joseph Simmons, a regular old witch, and fifteen others met up on Stone Mountain east of Atlanta. Stories say they read from a conjuring book inked in blood on human skin. Can't vouch for that. But it was them that called up the monsters we call Ku Kluxes. And it all started with this damned movie.

The Birth of a Nation comes from a book. Two books really—*The Clansman* and *The Leopard's Spots,* by a man named Thomas Dixon. Dixon's father was a South Carolina slaveowner in the Confederacy. And a sorcerer. Way I hear it, a heap of the big ups in the Confederacy was into sorcery. Dark stuff too. Jeff Davis, Bobby Lee, Stonewall Jackson—all in league with worse than the devil.

The first Klan started after the war. Nathan Bedford Forrest—another wicked conjurer—and some spiteful rebels sold their souls to the evil powers. Started calling themselves Night Riders. *Witches* is what the freed people named them. They talk about them first Klans having horns and looking like beasts! People think it's just Negro superstition. But some of them ex-slaves could *see* what Forrest and those hateful rebels had become. Monsters, like these Ku Kluxes.

Was freed people helped end that first Klan—Robert Smalls and his band. The Klans died out, but the evil they loosed lived on—whipping and killing colored people for voting, driving them from government, whole massacres that established this Jim Crow what still choking us now. Hard to tell who won the war and who lost.

For some, though, that wasn't enough.

Thomas Dixon's father was in the first Klan and taught him that dark sorcery. Dixon Jr. wrote his books as a conjuring: meant to deliver up the souls of readers to the evil powers, to bring the Klans back. But books could only reach so many. That's when D. W. Griffith took ahold of it. He and Dixon got to scheming and made over them books with a new kind of magic—the movie picture.

When *The Birth of a Nation* came out in 1915, papers carried on about how lifelike it was, like nothing nobody ever seen. It sold out week after week, month after month. Got shown to the Supreme Court, Congress, even at the White House. White folk ate up pictures of white men in black shoe polish chasing after white girls. Had white women swooning in their seats. Heard one time a white man pulled a pistol and shot up the screen—saying he trying to "rescue the fair damsel from that damned Negro brute." When the Klans ride in all gallant on their horses to save the day, white folk go wild—"like a people possessed," newspapers say, which ain't too far from the truth. Dixon and Griffith had made a conjuring that reached more people than any book could.

That same year, Simmons and his cabal met on Stone Mountain. *The Birth of a Nation* had delivered all the souls they needed to stir up them old evil powers. Across the country, white folk who ain't even heard of the Klan surrendered to the spell of them moving pictures. Got them believing the Klans the true heroes of the South, and colored people the monsters.

They say God is good all the time. Seem he also likes irony.

———

We leave downtown, driving past well-tended mansions on College Street and cross into Pleasant Hill—with its one-story farms, small bright-painted shotgun houses, and homes of well-to-do Negroes. Freed people settled Pleasant Hill close to College Street, so white folk could keep their cooks and maids near. Got its own lawyers, doctors, grocers, whatever you please—like a separate Macon.

Still, no telegraph lines though. The streets are unpaved, and the Packard kicks up dust in the dry July heat. Two years back, Pleasant Hill ran plumb out of water. Couldn't bathe babies, cook, clean. City moved slow as molasses in January to fix it. Only time they come here is when some Negro escapes a chain gang. Then Macon police ride in on motorbikes hemming everybody up.

We pass up a colored cemetery onto a long bend and down a bumpy stretch of road that make Sadie loose a string of complaints. Nana Jean's farm looks almost abandoned: with fields of bushes and potted plants. It ain't large: one story and a sloping roof supported by four posts, with a redbrick chimney and brown wood faded by sun and marked by rain. Only the front door stands out—a pale blue, like the porch ceiling and window frames.

Chef stops the Packard, and Sadie's already fussing for me to get moving. I don't even open the door before a face pokes out from a barn in the back, staring from behind welder's goggles. A body follows: a woman wearing a soot-stained gray welding apron over a white dress. She hikes up the hem and breaks into a stride in her laced-up black boots. Lord, that Choctaw woman can run! She's before us in the time it takes me to step down.

"You have it?" she pants, pulling up tinted goggles.

"And good day to you too, Molly," Chef greets, jumping out.

"Do you have it?" she asks again, round face frowning and all five feet of her drawing up. A gloved hand pushes strands of gray into a bonnet holding her hair. Molly Hogan is something of a scientist. And if she's anything to go on, they can be a one-minded lot.

"In the back," I answer. She follows me to where Chef is lifting up the canopy. In the bed, between two bales of cotton, sit big glass canisters full of murky liquid. One holds the head of a Ku Klux, its face smashed up against the inside. Another a hand, long claws and all. A third, much of a foot.

"I was hoping for an intact body," Molly says, inspecting the canisters like she at a meat shop.

"You ain't got nothing to fit a whole body," I remark.

"Are they at least still in their dormant phase?" *Dormant.* That what she call when a Ku Klux pretending to be human. Molly ain't got the sight. To her, what's preserved in that fluid is a man's severed head, hands, and feet—not a monster. Don't seem to bother her none. Scientists are strange.

"Didn't happen that way," I say. "And you welcome! Almost got killed getting these. We thought they was down but they got back up and sure wasn't *dormant* no more. Turned into a real fight!"

She looks up at me as if just noticing the mess I'm in. The edges of her eyes squint into tiny crow's feet. "Cordy's bomb didn't work?"

"My munitions was fine," Chef huffs.

Molly looks skeptical. "Should have been enough iron and silver in there—"

"Should've," Chef cuts in, "don't make it so."

Molly frowns up, then calls to the barn. Four women come running, all dressed like her but younger: one my age, one around Sadie's, and another just turned eighteen. Under Molly's instructions, they start gathering the canisters. It takes two to lift each. The oldest, her name Sarah, almost drops her end. Chef catches it quick and she blushes with thanks. Chef flashes a grin and she only blushes more. I elbow her right in the ribs.

"Oww! What?"

"We don't need that kind of trouble."

Chef chuckles, watching Sarah walk away. "Them hips ain't trouble at all."

We straighten as Molly turns to us. "What's with the cotton?"

Sadie, sitting on top of a bale, fishes out a bottle, wiggling it playfully.

"Whiskey!" Molly laughs. "How did you come by that?" Her look goes serious again. "Sorry about my earlier rudeness. Just a little out of sorts—got three distilleries going, not to mention my other work." She nods to the house. "Go on in and get some food. Call you when I'm ready for you."

She turns back to the barns, and we head to the house. Along the way we pass small trees with deep blue bottles on their branches, the hot summer wind making them whistle faintly. Like the door and porch ceiling, that blue's meant to ward off haints. Gullah folk say them bottles catch bad spirits. Can't see what that do to Ku Kluxes, but I ain't one to question Nana Jean's ways. From inside comes clapping and singing. The door is ajar and when we push it open, there's sights enough to catch your breath.

There's a Shout going on. In the center of the room, five men and women—their hair peppered with white—move in a backward circle to the song. Them's Shouters. Keeping time is the Stick Man, stooped and beating his cane on the floor. Behind him are three Basers—in overalls frayed by labor, and clapping hands just as worn. They cry out in answer to the Leader, a barrel-chested man named Uncle Will in a straw hat, bellowing out for the world to hear.

"Blow, Gabriel!"
"At the Judgment."
"Blow that trumpet!"
"At the Judgment bar."
"My God call you!"
"At the Judgment."
"Angels shouting!"
"At the Judgment bar."

The Shout come from slavery times. Though hear Uncle Will tell it, maybe it older than that. Slaves would Shout when they get some rest on Sundays. Or go off to the woods in secret. They'd come together and carry on like this: the Leader, the Stick Man, and the Basers, singing, clapping, and stamping, while the Shouters move to the song. In the Shout, you got to *move* the way the spirit tell you and can't stop until it let you go. And don't call it no dance! Not unless you want Uncle Will to set you down and learn you proper. See, the Shout ain't really the song, it's the *movement*. He say the Shouts like this one got the most power: about surviving slavery times, praying for freedom, and calling on God to end that wickedness.

I can feel my sword appear faint in my hand like a phantom thing—half in this world, half in another. The chanting in my head starts up, and chiefs and kings wail as those they sold flood to the leaf-shaped blade, and old gods stir awake to sway in time to the Shout. Whole room is flooded with light—rising up from the singers, crackling lightning bursting from the Stick Man's cane, and leaving dazzling tracks where the Shouter's feet shuffle without ever crossing. That brightness drowns out all else—even a frightened little girl whispering her fears before vanishing into smoke. My blade drinks in that magic, and the chanting in my head grows. But it don't just come to me. Most of that light flows to a woman in the center of the room in a haint-blue dress.

Nana Jean.

Magic washes up against her, long arms that look made of packed dark earth soaking up light. It oozes in fat drops from her fingertips into bottles arranged about her—and the liquid inside turns honey gold, lighting up like a lantern. I seen this Gullah woman do this plenty, and my eyes still wide.

When the Shout ends, the light vanishes. The Shouters, Basers, Stick Man, and Uncle Will covered in sweat, like they worked their spirits hard. Nana Jean drops down to plop heavy into a chair, her fleshy body creaking the wood as young boys cork the bottles and pack them into crates.

This here Nana Jean's secret recipe—parts corn, barley liquor, and Gullah root magic. For some it's a drink—smooth as gin, strong as whiskey. Others use it to sanctify homes. Or to rub down babies. Folk call it all kinds of things: Mama's Tears, Pure Water, Mami's Wata. But each bottle got the name in plain letters: Mama's Water.

Nana Jean intend it as protection. A bit of magic to ward off evil in our times—Klans, lynching, mobs. And Ku Kluxes. Maybe it do, maybe it don't. But this concoction one of the biggest moneymakers in the county. When me, Sadie, and Chef ain't chasing Ku Kluxes, we running Mama's Water across half of Georgia. Like I said, this monster-hunting business don't pay for itself.

The scent of food coming from a table makes my mouth water. People already about it, heaping up plates. I'm set to join them when I feel Nana Jean's gaze calling. I sigh.

Look like food gon' have to wait. I turn, stepping through the crowd toward her.

This old woman the reason I'm in Macon now. Was three years back I heard her call, way up in Memphis, a croon riding the wind like dandelion seeds in that Red Summer. Reached me when I was running through the Tennessee woods: half-mad, blade in hand, exacting what vengeance on Ku Kluxes I could *for what they done.* Sadie the same way, tearing red death through Alabama with Winnie after Ku Kluxes murdered her grandpappy. Cordy came back from the war to Harlem, then Chicago, running from nightmares, claiming she could see monsters. But Nana Jean bid us stop, to turn our ears to her and come. Recruited us as soldiers in this war.

"Nana Jean," I greet respectful.

She stay seated in her big chair. Her crinkly white hair hangs to her shoulders, almost as bushy as mine when it ain't tied down. The scent of tilled country earth fills the space between us as brown-gold eyes look me over. She stops at my right hand, frowning. My sword is gone, but I know them eyes can trace its ghostly residue. She don't approve of the blade. Or where it come from. Say gifts from haints carry a price. But she got her magic. And I got mine.

"Dem buckrah debbil gii hunnuh trouble?" she asks.

Nana Jean was raised up Gullah though she been in Macon most her life. Say her people bound to them Carolina islands, and being away so long faded her a bit. Though her Gullah talk don't sound faded none.

I relate what happened and her bushy eyebrows jump like white caterpillars. "Hunnuh jook dat buckrah debbil fuh see if e been dead?"

My turn to frown. "I know a dead Ku Klux from a living one. That silver and iron hit them, and they get right back up."

She sucks her teeth. "Ki! Buckrah debbil dem ain good fuh nuttin!" Then more sober: "If dat silva ain good fuh nuttin needuh, dat real trouble fuh true. Lawd hep wi."

"Nothing we can't handle." Brave words, but I share her uneasiness.

"Hunnuh ain kill no fool buckrah?"

Buckrah devils what she calls Ku Kluxes. *Fool buckrah* she reserves for Klans who ain't *turned*. She very particular about us not killing them who still human. Say every sinner got a chance to get right. I suppose. Way I see it, one less Klan, one less chance of a Ku Klux. But I bides by her rules and shake my head.

She nods back, eyes wandering to the Shouters. Uncle Will talking to a small woman in a plain dress brown as her tied-up hair—the German widow, Emma Krauss. Her husband owned a store in town but the flu took him in 1918. She still have the store and is mixed up in our bootlegging business. But in Germany she trained to study music and can't get enough of the Shout. Spends time writing down their songs and asking on how they come about.

"When this lot heading home?"

Nana Jean grumbles. "Say dey da gwine Friday. Fraid

dey biggity preacha. E say de root haffa do wit witchcraft."
She snorts. "Biggity down preacha."

That ain't good. Shouters needed for brewing Mama's
Water. Only lots say it's wrong mixing up roots with the
Shout. Sure ain't for the bootlegging. Nana Jean argue better to keep folk alive; worry on their souls later. She convinced Uncle Will, mostly because he sweet on her.

"But mebbe dey stay fah nyam me bittle." She winks.
The mention of food whips up a hunger that must show on
my face. "Go git uh plate fore dat po' gyal nyam up all me
bittle!"

Don't need to look to know she's talking about Sadie. Girl
could eat a whole cow, and God only know where she puts
it. I turn to go, but Nana Jean catches my arm. I look to find
her face thundering, brown-gold eyes bright like the sun.

"Las' night, uh yeddy three rooster singing at de moon!"
she whispers. "Dis morning uh see uh rat swalluh up uh
snake big dey, big dey! Me dream dem full uh blood redhead buckrah man. Dem omen bad. Bad, bad, bad. Yo tit-
tuh dem." She jerks a wobbly chin at Sadie and Chef. "Mine
one'nuddah. Dis time yuh a ebil time. Bad wedduh gwine
come."

When she lets go and falls back, I realize I been holding
my breath. What in the blazes was that about? But the Gullah woman already closed her eyes, humming soft. I shake
off the cold gripping my bones and head to join the others.

By the time I grab a plate and sit down, I'm famished!
There's oyster rice, spicy shrimp and grits, fried okra,

roasted fish, and sweet salty corn cakes. Take all my home training not to lick my fingers clean. Beside me, Sadie moans, rubbing her belly as across from us, Chef and the German widow argue up a storm.

"What they going on about?" I ask.

"What they always going on about?" Sadie replies.

She picks up a New York tabloid—Emma has them delivered to her store—with pictures recalling the 1920 Wall Street bombing, and hands me a small pamphlet. It got a drawing of three men—colored, white, maybe Chinese—swinging hammers at a chained globe. WORKERS OF THE WORLD UNITE! it reads. One of Emma's for sure. Chef don't care much for it, what she call Bolshevik rantings.

"And I don't want to see colored folk as shock troops in your revolution," she's insisting. "This ain't Moscow."

"Nein," Emma responds. "But there exist all the inequities of the tsar's Russia. Sharecroppers like serfs. The debasement of workers. Race prejudice. All which socialism would eradicate!"

"Socialism going to solve white folk?"

"Once the poor white worker sees his commonality with the colored—"

Chef laughs. "Your poor white workers be the first ones at a lynching. Up in Chicago they chase colored folk from their unions." She leans in. "When I was small, white folk rioted because Jack Johnson outboxed a white man on the Fourth of July. They hunted Negroes from New York to

Omaha. Slit a colored man's throat on a streetcar, just for saying who won the fight. You think Marx can fix that?"

Emma frowns. She ten years older than me, though hard to tell with her small features behind those round spectacles. "We must strive to show them they too are exploited. And not by those they are taught to hate, from which they earn nothing."

"Oh see, I disagree," Chef retorts. "White folk earn something from that hate. Might not be wages. But knowing we on the bottom and they set above us—just as good, maybe better."

"But can you not imagine a better society?" Emma pleads. "Where colored and white work for the greater good? Where women are the equal of men? I did not support the Great War—it being a capitalist venture. But you fought. Yet you had to do so playing the part of a man, to join these Harlem Hayfighters."

"Hellfighters," Chef corrects.

"Ach! My point remains, we must dare to imagine a more equal world."

Chef shakes her head. "Imagining a thing don't make it so. Me, I say let Negroes hoard up money like white folk been doing; let us get a few Rockefellers and Carnegies. My people got enough troubles without getting tied up with Bolsheviks. Ever think maybe *your* people might fare better if you wasn't going around touting communism?"

Emma puts on a sad smile that pokes dimples in her

cheeks. "My people make money and we are 'greedy capitalists.' We call for an equitable society, and we are 'dirty Bolsheviks.' Those who wish to hate Jews will always find justification. They hung poor Mr. Frank here in Georgia after all, despite reason or the law."

Chef grunts. "Reason and law don't mean much when white folk want their way."

I turn from their conversation, putting aside the pamphlet and pulling out my book. It's bent up and creased, but the front still visible—*NEGRO FOLKTALES*. I flip it open and let the words drown out the world until Sadie nudges me.

"How many times you read that thing already?"

I shrug. "Never kept count."

"You ain't got no new books?"

"It was my brother's." First time I tell anybody that.

"Oh. He write it?"

"No. But he used to read it to me."

"Stories 'bout Bruh Rabbit and Bruh Bear?"

"And Bruh Lion and Tar Baby . . ."

A smile tugs my lips remembering his voice, all excited in the telling.

"Grandpappy had stories," Sadie says. "Not no talking animals. Stories of haint lights, river witches, and people who could fly. He say slaves from Africy had wings, but white folk cut them off so they couldn't fly home. When I was little, he say my mama fly away like that. Took me a while to know he mean she run off."

Sadie's mama used to clean some big white man's house back in Alabama. One day he get to watching her close and he . . . well, he done a very bad thing. After her mama leave, her grandpappy raise her. He never say who her daddy was, on account of Sadie being good with a rifle and Sadie being . . . well, Sadie. She catch my look and shrug in them too-big overalls.

"Maybe my mama did spread wings and fly like a bird. Gone where she can't be hurt no more. I ain't mad at her for that."

She says that as casual as relating the time. But there's a hitch in her voice that tell me she carrying her hurt deep, the way we all do. In my head, I remember my own mama, her humming lulling me to sleep and filling up the morning. Me and my brother would just lie around listening, drinking her voice in.

"What we doing tonight?" Sadie asks, switching topics.

"Nana Jean got a run for us, maybe."

"Pfft! On the Fourth of July? Bet your man's joint gon' be jumping!"

"Oh?" I return to my book.

"Oh? Best you got is an Oh? We running Mama's Water for two weeks. Come right back to hunt Ku Kluxes. And you ain't thinking on him?"

"Maybe I is, or I ain't."

A long wicked Sadie chuckle follows. "I had a man fine like that, I wouldn't be thinking on riding around running Mama's Water. I'd be thinking about riding his—"

"Sadie Watkins!" I exclaim, looking up in exasperation.

"Don't be no prude. What you think Nana Jean and Uncle Will doing up in here tonight—"

"Sadie! I'm asking you to stop. Please!"

She's grinning like a cat with no such intentions, when her eyes move behind me. I turn to find Nana Jean herself coming our way, one of Molly Hogan's apprentices in tow. We stand up when she reaches us, and even Chef breaks off her debate.

"Molly dem ready fuh see we," the Gullah woman says.

"You can see the epidermis has grown a second sheath."

We in one of the barns that serve as Molly's laboratory, watching her cut open the arm of a Ku Klux. Her gloved fingers peel back pale skin, showing muscle that turns gray as one of her apprentices douses it in preserving fluid that drips down the wood table.

"Notice also the hand, the claws becoming more prehensile, almost feline."

She wipes at her face, forgetting it's under a metal helmet—only her eyes peeking behind smoky glass. Molly ain't got the sight. Few do. So she built this contraption, which her apprentices charge by cranking a metal wheel. It allows her to see like us—or something close.

"You saying this Ku Klux turning into a cat?" Chef asks.

"I'm saying that the organism—the Ku Klux—is evolving."

"Evolving?" Sadie looks up, fiddling with the knobs of a microscope. "Like that monkey man's book?"

"Darwin," Molly answers, pulling the microscope away.

"He the one. But you say that take a long time."

Molly looks impressed Sadie remembers. "It's supposed to. But I've recorded these changes over months. They're happening, and fast."

Molly been making a study of Ku Kluxes. She the one ask us to bring back specimens. Say she always had a head full of smart. Only, wasn't no school for freed people in Choctaw country in Oklahoma, so she taught herself. Came to Macon at Nana Jean's calling, and brung her apprentices too. They brew up Mama's Water in the other barn, and use this one for experimenting.

"But what does it mean?" Emma asks, eyeing the Ku Klux arm like it might bite.

Molly swings up the helmet, mopping her forehead.

"Choctaw that owned my parents were Baptists. But my mother learned the old religion from those that refused the missionaries. Said they believe in three worlds—where we live, an Above world, and a Below world, full of other beings."

Sadie smirks. "Thought you was a godless atheist."

"I am. But who's to say our universe is alone? Maybe there's others stacked beside us like sheets of paper. And these Ku Kluxes crossed over from somewhere else."

"They was conjured," Chef reminds.

"'Conjuring' is just a way to open a door. Explains why their anatomy is so different, and the extreme reactions to our elements."

"Why they like drinking water so," Sadie adds.

She right on that. Can tell a Ku Klux straight away by all the water they drink. Colored folk who lived through them first Klans say they'd empty whole buckets, claiming they was the ghosts of soldiers from Shiloh. *More water,* they'd demand. *Just come from hell, and plenty dry.*

"That too," Molly says. "But they're changing, right down to their organs, adapting to our world."

"Like they planning to stay," I finish.

Molly nods, and the room goes quiet.

"That's how the government want it," Sadie speaks into the silence. "Y'all can roll your eyes all you want! But I'm telling you the government know 'bout all this. Been experimenting on them Ku Kluxes just like Molly. Can't say if they working with them or against, but they know!"

Sadie got it in her head the Warren G. Harding government knows about Ku Kluxes. Say she pieced it together from the tabloids. That Woodrow Wilson was in on Griffith's plan, but it got out of hand. And now there's secret departments come about since the war, who go around studying Ku Kluxes. Girl got some imagination.

"Wherever these things from," Chef grumbles, "they mighty active of late."

She turns to a map pinned to a barn wall. Red dots mark it, indicating Klan activity. Two years back was only a few dots, most here in Georgia. Now there's red everywhere— through the South, swallowing the Midwest, going far up as Oregon.

"Mrs. Wells-Barnett's intel say Klan chapters on the rise," Chef notes.

"And how many are Ku Kluxes?" Emma asks, eyeing the sea of red.

Molly shakes her head. "We haven't been able to gauge that. Once infected, morphological transformation seems dependent on the individual."

That's science talk for how Klan folk turn Ku Klux. Molly says it's like an infection, or a parasite. And it feed on hate. She says chemicals in the body change up when you hate strong. When the infection meets that hate, it starts growing until it's powerful enough to turn the person Ku Klux. Ask me, it's plain evil them Klans let in, eating them up until they hollow inside. Leave behind bone-white demons who don't remember they was men.

"Not to mention," Molly continues, "they're rereleasing that movie."

We all go sour at that. Seven years since *The Birth of a Nation* first come out—raising up hate enough to make these Ku Kluxes. Now that wicked D. W. Griffith set to release it again. Suddenly, I remember the poster.

"They're showing it Sunday, at Stone Mountain."

Everybody looks at me and I explain.

"Stone Mountain," Emma murmurs. "Where Simmons did his conjuring."

"That movie, what you call a spell, I believe, works to induce hate on a mass scale," Molly says. "Like how a lynching riles individuals into a mob."

Sadie scoffs. "Then why come it only *riles* white folk?"

"Whatever the case," Molly continues, "these Ku Kluxes are born from that hate. If the rerelease of Griffith's film has the same effect as before, we could be looking at an epidemic. Possibly worse than 1919."

Chef whispers a curse before I can get one out; 1919 was a hard year for all of us.

"You think them Klans dress up to look like Ku Kluxes?" Sadie asks. She's bent down now, eyeballing the head stuffed into glass. "It white like they hoods, and got a pointy end. Anyway, I say we just blow up some theater houses where the movie's showing. Like Trotter did in Boston back in '15."

"Mr. Trotter *did not* blow up a movie house," Emma corrects. "He only set off a smoke bomb to clear the theater. The riot started after."

"Well, let's blow one up for real," Sadie insists. "For white folks' own good, and ours, since they can't see what's right under they noses. Monsters all up between them and not a one got the sight!"

"I can see," Emma reminds.

Sadie stands up, frowning. "Jews is white folk?"

Emma fumbles for words, but Nana Jean cuts in. "Buckrah dem done been waak 'longside de debbil long nuf fuh know'um. Dey jes ain wahn fuh see."

Molly clears her throat. "Why some can see the creatures and others can't is a question for science. More important, we should consider my other theory."

"Your notion there is an intelligence guiding these dämonen?" Emma asks.

Molly nods. "The Ku Kluxes behave like worker ants—spreading the colony. So who's directing them? There must be some hierarchy we don't yet understand."

"We only ever seen Ku Kluxes," Chef says. "And they ain't got much sense."

"Sense enough to spread all over," Sadie mutters.

My eyes are pulled back to the map. I ain't put much into Molly's talk of some brain controlling Ku Kluxes. But all that red reminds me of a chessboard, and the other pieces closing in.

"If as we believe East St. Louis in 1917 was a prelude to 1919," Molly presses, "then what do we make of Tulsa? A massive coordinated attack. Our defenses overrun in days—"

"We remember," Chef interrupts. The whole barn feel colder at the mention. We ain't the only ones fighting this war. There's pockets of resistance all over—Eatonsville, Charleston, Houston. But losing Tulsa last year was a hard blow. I can still see Ku Kluxes marching, clawing through all the fire and smoke.

"What are you saying?" Emma asks, brown eyes full of worry.

Molly draws a breath. "The growth of Klan chapters, the creatures' adaptations, the organized attacks, now the re-release of that film. If there's an intelligence behind this—and I believe there is—we're on the verge of something big. Be ready."

I glance to Nana Jean, who standing with her arms folded, face hard as stone as she stares at the Ku Klux arm on the table. In my head, seems I can hear the hot July wind whistling through those bottle trees outside, singing her words.

Bad wedduh, bad wedduh, bad wedduh, gwine come . . .

Notation 32:

There's a Shout we call *Rock Daniel.* Now Daniel was a slave always stealing from massa's store-house. Nobody tell. They like getting that meat too. And Daniel's stealing not no real sin—not when the first set of stealing was they who stole us from Africy. One time, he stealing just as massa coming to the storehouse. The slaves start singing loud to warn him! When we do that Shout, we tell Daniel to "move" and "rock"—to slip past massa's whip [laughter]! Even in the wickedest times, you got to find some enjoyment. Or you not gon' survive.

—Interview with Jupiter "Sticker" Woodberry, age seventy, transliterated from the Gullah by EK

THREE

The music at Frenchy's so loud I feel it on my insides. The piano man up out his seat, one leg hanging off the grainy wood and pounding the keys hard enough to break them. He sweating so I'm wondering how that shiny conk holding up. Whole while he wailing on about some big-boned woman he left in New Orleans, just about jumping out his maroon suit to croon, "And when she roll that jelly!" The crowd roars, men whooping and women fanning hands like to cool him off.

Frenchy's Inn not the only colored spot in Macon. But tonight it's the one to be at. Most here is sharecroppers and laborers. Every table packed. Where there ain't tables people on their feet, roosted on the stairs—fitting in however. Hardly room to dance or a patch of quiet to think. Whole place is a hot, sweltering, haze-of-July-in-Georgia mess. But long as the liquor pouring and the music going, everybody right as rain.

Sadie called it. No bootlegging tonight. Nana Jean bid us step out, even if she ain't one for "de jook jaint nonsense." Frenchy's not no regular juke joint, though—no shotgun shack what got leaks in the roof. It's a full two stories and an inn for colored travelers, nice enough so folk wear their best—which ain't much for laborers and sharecroppers. But me and my set, we step out in style.

I traded in my knickers for a marigold dress beaded with embroidery that glitters in the light of kerosene lamps. Chef dressed down in a dark plaid, rust-colored suit with an orange bow tie, looking like she walked right off Harlem's streets. Even got Sadie out of them overalls and into a red lace chemise gown. Don't look half-bad on her skinny self, even while she up on our table whistling at the piano man. When he finishes to cheers she climbs down to fall into her seat.

"Hard to believe your grandpappy was a preacher," Chef calls over.

Sadie snorts, flicking back her long braid. "It ain't Sunday. Grandpappy, rest his soul, won't mind none." She picks up a bottle of Mama's Water before opting for the pilfered whiskey, pouring it heavy in our glasses.

"Oh, that's enough for me, Miss Sadie!" a thickset man says. That there's Lester, a Macon local who always finds his way to us, or more properly to Sadie. She like her men husky, and the two fooled around some months back. But she got this rule of not spending the night with the same man twice. Say otherwise they get to thinking stupid. Whatever she put on Lester, though, left him nose open, and he been trying to court her since. Some men just like trouble.

"Lester Henry," she says in a tone hot enough to lay

down your baby hairs. "You betta move that hand from on top your glass 'fore I move it for you. This a juke joint, not no temperance revival!"

Lester's smile slides away, drooping his meaty jowls. But he moves his hand.

Chef barks a laugh. She got an arm around Bessie, another local who remind me of the big-boned woman from the song. Her ruby-painted fingernails trace lazy lines through the part in Chef's short-trimmed hair and the two lean into each other in the way of lovers rediscovering their familiarity. The sight send my own eyes wandering, until they land on the finest thing in the room.

Michael George—who folk call Frenchy. On account of his creole talk.

He come from St. Lucia. Left home when he was sixteen, looking to find work on Roosevelt's Panama Canal. Only when he get there it was done already. So he started traveling. Been through the West Indies, South America, and whereabouts. Come up to Florida and kept moving, settling in Macon and opening up this spot. Claim it's a mix of a Mississippi juke joint, rum shops they got in St. Lucia, and spots he seen in Cuba. Say poor folk deserve some fanciness too.

He standing near the bar—tall and good looking. I can make out the trace of his shoulders under the high-collared striped shirt and ivory suit jacket that fit just right on his dark skin. I'm remembering what he look like with it off too. There's this spot, where his leg meet his waist, that's a perfect *V,* and I imagine my fingers strumming it . . .

"Maryse, what you over there smiling about?"

I turn to find Sadie eyeing me, and sip my whiskey. Was I smiling?

"You best go get that man 'fore one of them gals try to hitch him." She nods to a cluster of women around him. "Know good and well that your man. Probably bad-mouthing us too."

Maybe so. Folk in Macon have peculiar ideas about us. Say we witches, like they whisper Nana Jean is. You'd think lady bootleggers was scandalous enough.

Sadie leans close. "You want me to bust up one of them heffas?" Her nostrils flare and the air prickles. She mean it too. Don't mind our fussing and carrying on. Sadie will tear up this whole joint if she catch whiff somebody out to hurt me or Chef. It's sweet, in a crazy way.

"Sadie Watkins, I ain't never fought over no man and not starting today."

"Gal, don't go starting trouble," Bessie warns. "Wasn't for Maryse, Frenchy might not have let you back up in here *after last time.*"

Sadie rolls her eyes. But she settles back and I breathe easy. Chef glances my way, mouthing, *Stop playing with dynamite!*

We're saved when Lester starts up on his favorite topic— Marcus Garvey. He traveled up north once and come back with a head full of Garvey. Even sells UNIA newspapers here in Macon. Why he thinks that might impress Sadie I got no idea.

I look back to Michael George to find his eyes lingering on me above the heads of the women about him. He smiles pretty, like I'm the only other person here, like he's seeing me again for the first time when we met a year back. Same smile he had on when we walked through the door tonight, catching me in a hug. The solid feel of him still in my head, drinking in his familiar scent mingled with shaving cream. We ain't get to talk long, just some assurances of later before he set us up at a table. But the heat of his look right now makes my belly flutter, and I'm wondering how long *later* might be? Somebody calls to him, taking his eyes away, and I'm plunged back into the conversation going on about me.

"And that's why Mr. Garvey says the Negro has to go back to Africa, to claim what's ours." Leave it up to Lester to talk politics in a juke joint.

Sadie seems like she only half listening, but then declares, "I say we go to Europe. See how they like getting carved up—beat up as they is after the war."

Lester blinks, but picks up quick. He's used to how Sadie's mind works.

"Well, Miss Sadie, Mr. Garvey say let Europe be for the Europeans and Africa for the Africans. That way we make a home for ourselves."

"I got a home right here," Chef says, lighting a Chesterfield. "Bled and fought for it. Still fighting. I ain't going nowhere."

"Won't argue that," Lester says. "But we could do great

things in Africa. Restore the colored race to our greatness, like in times past."

"What you mean, greatness in times past?" Sadie asks, pouring more whiskey.

"I'm meaning the time colored people ruled the world."

Sadie squints. "Colored folk ruled the world? When that happen?"

"You ain't read that in your tabloids?" Chef snarks.

"Oh yes, Miss Sadie! The old Negro empires in ancient times. There's this colored woman in Oklahoma, Drusilla Houston? She writing a book on how the Ethiopians and Cushites was the first people on Earth. She say at one time the whole world was colored and—"

"If the whole world was colored," Sadie interjects, "how white folk come about?"

Lester looks stumped, but recovers quick. "Well, some say white folk was the first albinos. But I don't think it so. I read that book by that fella on evolution—"

"Darwin!" Sadie exclaims. "I know him!"

"Yes! Well, Darwin say animals change over time. So I'm thinking, why not people? Maybe white folk was colored, and they got paler like they do when they get scared. Or cold. You ain't never seen white folk pale like they got up north. Either they scared all the time or it's the cold."

For a while Sadie says nothing, glass held to her lips but not drinking. That means she turning something big over in her head. When she talks, it's almost a whisper.

"You telling me, white folk is niggers?"

That leaves Lester speechless.

Chef shakes her head. "Lord, you done started something now."

"Well, Miss Sadie . . . I suppose . . . Not how I would put it . . ."

"White folk is niggers!" Sadie repeats, slamming her glass hard enough to make Lester jump. "This whole time, they putting on and acting high and mighty! But they just niggers who stayed in the cold too long! Bet that's why they so mean. Know deep down they come out that same jungle—that the nigger they made up in their heads right under they own skin! Oh, fix your face, Maryse, I'm using the small *n*." She fills up Lester's glass and thrusts it at him. "Tell me more about these Cushees—"

"Cushites," he corrects.

"Yeah, them. I want to know all about this long-ago time when the world was colored." She sips her whiskey slow. "Talk right and I just might break my rule."

Lester sits straight up like his number just hit.

I'm wondering how I'm going to endure the coming conversation when the twang of a guitar sounds, chased by a harmonica's whine. The piano man back on his keys, and a lady in a white dress next to him starts clapping and singing. Her voice rides the air strong as a current, lifting folk off their feet. Seem the whole joint is up at once, pairing off and pulling partners into a space opened up for dancing. Chef and Bessie are gone before I can blink. Sadie and Lester follow, though she come back to snatch the whiskey bottle, leaving me alone. Well, that won't do.

Downing my whiskey, I get to my feet, maneuvering through hugged-up bodies and swaying hips, all shedding the pain, labors, and trials of their days. A few men—long past drunk—try to stop me, but I slip away easy. The one fool that grabs my arm, I set a look on him so fierce he don't know if I'm God or the devil, and he lets go quick.

I find Michael George still near the bar, two women trying to entice him to dance. When he sees me, he excuses himself, leaving them to pout.

"You just gon' have me sitting at that table like some old maid?"

He smiles. "You with your friends dem. I doh want to bother you."

"I'll let you know when you bothering me," I answer, stepping closer. His arms slip around my waist and without another word that music snatches us up, willing us to lose ourselves to it, like it got its own magic. For a brief moment all thoughts of Ku Kluxes and bad premonitions fade away. So that there's nothing but the music and all of us being baptized in its healing. It's more than I can take.

I reach up to whisper, "You need somebody else to lock up." He looks at me one time before signaling to the bartender. Love I ain't got to tell him twice, and I'm already pulling him up the stairs.

By the time we reach his room, we done stopped to trade

breathy kisses half a dozen times, hands slipping into and out of each other's clothes, undoing things and treading across skin. Whole time he begging like a man starving.

"Maryse girl. I miss you too bad. You mustn't leave so again. Promise me nah?"

I don't make promises. But I plan to let him know just how much I missed him. He barely gets the door closed before I'm pulling off his vest, his shirt, trying not to break a button. Don't recall how I end up on top the tiger oak tallboy, pressed against the mirror, marigold dress pushed to my waist. He unbuttoning his pants when I stop him.

"Been a long two weeks and a hell of a day. I need you to do that thing."

He runs a precious tongue on his teeth. "You doh even have to ask."

When he makes to bend down, I stop him again. "And talk that creole talk."

That pretty smile again. "Wi. Chansè pou mwen, mwen enmen manjè èpi mwen enmen palè. Kitè mwen di'w on sigwè . . ."

I got no idea what he saying, but it make every bit of me tingle. I will my mind to go easy, listening to the music downstairs, whispering his name and telling him how bad I need this. When his lips start up that creole talk between my thighs, I arch my back and do my own set of singing.

I know I'm dreaming. Because I'm wearing fighting clothes— shirt, knickers, gaiters, and Oxfords. And standing in my old house. It's always night here. All night forever. The house is a cabin outside Memphis. Year after the Civil War, white folk in Memphis went wild, lynching any colored man in blue for a soldier, burning colored houses and schools. My great-granddaddy escaped by leaving his Union uniform behind. Built a house way out here, fleeing that terror and white folks' madness.

It just like I left it, seven years back, looking like a whirlwind passed through. Ain't but one room, and I step over furniture and broken pots, kneeling down to lay my ear to the floor. Breathing comes, fast and deep. I trace fingers along the floorboards to catch fine grooves, lifting the almost unseen hatch.

The girl staring up at me got my eyes, though be a while before she grows into them. She shaking so hard under her nightshirt I can hear her teeth chattering, and the fear rolling off her stank enough I can taste its bitter. I push it back, studying her rounded lips, how the edges of her nose flares, the fat round her cheeks, and the way her plaited hair blends into the black of the small space. Like looking into a mirror of yesterdays.

"Not enough you bothering me when I gotta fight, now you in my dreams too?"

She just whimpers. I grit my teeth, disgusted.

"You ain't got to be scared. You got that sword."

Her little knuckles tighten around the silver hilt at her side. But she don't even try to lift it. That makes me madder still.

"Get on up outta here! You too grown for all this!"

A squeak escapes her lips and she stammers. "What if they come back?"

"They not coming back!" I'm shouting now. "You just gon' sit here! Getting filthy! You coulda done something with that sword! You coulda tried to stop them! Damn you, why won't you get out of here! Why don't you leave me alone!"

Something in her face changes, chasing the fright away, and her voice goes smooth as water.

"Same reason you won't go into the barn out back. We know what scare us. Don't we, Maryse?"

I suck in breath, and some of her fear slides down my throat.

She looks herself over. "Why you always imagine me as a girl? We wasn't so. You thinking this put more distance between us?"

"What do you want?" I plead.

"To tell you they watching. They like the places where we hurt. They use it against us."

They? "Who you talking about?"

The fear reappears like a mask, and her voice drops to a whisper. "They coming!"

In a blink, the world is swallowed in blackness. I panic, thinking I'm back in the hideaway place under the floors, raw fright threatening to take hold. But no, this not my house. I turn in a circle, searching that impenetrable darkness, when something catches my ear. Is that singing?

A faint light appears ahead I know wasn't there before. But it's where the noise is coming from. I walk toward it and as I do, the light takes shape into something. Or someone. A man. I can see him from the back—wide and broad like a motor truck, with a melon for a head topped in red hair. He wearing a white shirt and black pants held up by suspenders, with something tied about him I think is an apron. Can't make out what he's doing, but he's bent over, swinging one arm, and each time it come down there's a wet *THUNK*! Then a little *squeal!* He the one singing—or trying to. Making the most godawful racket, all off pitch and off beat. Take me a while to recognize the words.

"And when she roll that jelly!"

He chuckles. *THUNK! Squeal!*

"We like that one," he says in a deep Georgia drawl. "But don't understand." *THUNK! Squeal!* "What does she roll like jelly? Is it made of real jelly? Sticky and sweet?" *THUNK! Squeal!* "Here, we know another one." He clears his throat and starts to caterwauling:

Oh, the grand old Duke of York,
He had ten thousand men!
He marched them up to the top of the hill,
And he marched them down again.
And when they're up, they're up,
And when they're down, they're down.
And when they're only halfway up,
They're neither up nor down!

He chuckles again, and I catch a whiff of something rancid.

"That one we understand. Up, down. Up, down. But jelly?"

THUNK! THUNK! Squeal! Squeal!

I can't say why, but I want to see what he doing. I scoot to the side, trying not to get too close, and catch a glimpse of his hands. Big burly things. He got thick thumbs wrapped around the wood hilt of a silver cleaver and he's hacking up meat on a bloodstained table. Only every time he cut a piece, it inches away, a small hole opening up on it I realize is a mouth. And it squeals.

THUNK the cleaver go.

Squeal! the meat lets out.

I rear back in disgust, and he turns about to face me.

He as big in the front as the back, a thick and solid man. He hooks his cleaver on a loop at his waist, and I can see a matching one on the other side. His mouth opens into a too-wide grin on a shaved face and he wipes bloody smears on his white apron before extending a hand.

Realizing I ain't shaking that thing, he lowers it.

"Well, we finally get to meet you, Maryse."

I grimace at hearing my name. "You know me?"

He grins wider. "Oh, we been watching you a long time, Maryse. A long time."

"Who you, then? Some wicked haint messing with my dreams?"

He winks a gray eye. "We the storm on the horizon. But

you can call us Clyde—Butcher Clyde. We thought we'd introduce ourselves proper, since you gone and left this nice little space open for us to slip into."

Storm. Nana Jean's words play in my head. *Bad wedduh gwine come.*

"Well, you can slip yourself right back out," I snap.

He laughs a deep belly laugh. And I swear his stomach moves under that apron.

"We really going to have to dance, Maryse. You just bring that sword of yours next time, you hear? Don't worry, we'll bring the music." He extends his arms and starts up singing again. "Oh, the grand old Duke of York, He had ten thousand men . . . !"

As he do, little holes break out across his skin. On the exposed parts of his hairy arms, up on his neck, all along his round face. They're mouths, I realize with a shudder— small mouths with tiny jagged teeth fitted into red gums. All as one they start singing too, joining him in the worst chorus you ever heard. No harmony or rhythm, just a hundred voices crashing together.

> *And when they're up, they're up,*
> *And when they're down, they're down.*
> *And when they're only halfway up,*
> *They're neither up nor down!*

I cover my ears. Because this, whatever it is, don't dare call it music, *hurts!* In desperation I try to call up my sword, but can't get my mind right. It's like everything is off, the whole world spinning, and I stumble, trying to catch my balance. He just stands there laughing and singing, all those little mouths laughing and singing too. His hands grab his apron, tearing it off and ripping open his shirt. The skin on his pale belly ripples and peels back to reveal a pit of emptiness. No, not emptiness. Another mouth—big enough to eat me whole! With sharp teeth long as fingers and a flicking red tongue!

"We still want our dance, Maryse!" that mouth growls.

He jumps at me, and I swing a fist only to have my arm sink into his chest. His whole body—clothes and all—done turned pitch black, liquid and oozing. The mouths still there too, opening and closing with wet sucking hisses.

I kick out and a leg goes into him, sticking me fast.

Like how Tar Baby catch Bruh Rabbit! my brother wails.

Butcher Clyde laughs, and his tongue flies like a ribbon, wrapping round my middle. I try to peel the nasty fleshy thing off, but it's so damn strong, dragging me closer, toward that awful mouth, open wide—waiting.

I jump awake, breathing heavy and don't mind saying scared as shit! But there's no tongue wrapped about me. No Tar Baby man with a mouth in his belly. The echo of that terrible singing still in my ears, though. I let it fade and focus on my surroundings.

I can hear Sadie, loud as hell in a nearby room with

Lester, and I don't know who making more noise between the two. She the one cussing up a storm, but pretty certain he doing all the moaning.

Chef here too, whimpering somewhere as Bessie makes shushing whispers. She gets like this sometimes. Starts apologizing to dead men, then wakes up sobbing. Like a piece of that war come home with her. Sometimes I wonder what would have happened if my brother went off to that war, and what he might have brung back.

Other than them, just the sound of Georgia crickets in the night, telling me the juke joint closed up, except for those who want a room and some alone time. I turn to gaze at Michael George beside me, naked as the day he was born and finer than frog hair. I pull closer to nuzzle his neck, smelling the lingering cigar smoke, a habit he picked up in Havana. Two of us like to sit around after, sharing one and talking. Well, he do most of the talking. Not that he ain't curious—seems like he got a hundred questions about me. None I'm ready to answer. Beyond bootlegging, not much to tell. He ain't got the sight. And monster hunting's hard to explain. He know by the way I go quiet not to ask about my past or my family. Some things not for saying.

Besides, I prefer his stories of far-off places with white beaches and haint-blue waters. He tell me of a place named Tulum. Says at night on the ocean, the stars so plentiful, look like they just falling into the sea. Says he wants to take me there. That the two of us could get a boat, and just sail the whole world round. Sometimes I let myself imagine what that would be like. No more Ku Kluxes or fighting, just me and him and all that water. Think it'd be like freedom.

I squint at a sudden glare, forcing me out my thoughts. I raise up to find my sword propped in a corner, glowing bright. I didn't call it, so it being here mean I'm wanted. So much for dreaming about freedom. I disentangle from Michael George, who shifts his weight but don't wake. Grabbing up his shirt, I slip it on and hop out the bed, walking to my sword and grabbing it by the hilt . . . then stumble as the room falls away. I shake off a bout of dizziness and glance around. I'm standing in a green field under a bright blue sky, only there's no sun.

This ain't no dream, though. And I'm not alone.

There's three women. Two are older, sitting in fancy high-backed chairs at a white table beneath the biggest Southern red oak you ever seen. Both got the knowing looks of aunties, which is what I call them. The third, she on a swing hanging by a rope from the tree and gliding back and forth. Her face young enough to be my sister, but she's pure auntie, no mistaking. All three got on canary-yellow dresses with lace and embroidery, set off by colorful wide-brimmed hats. One at the table looks up from where she's stirring a glass pitcher.

"Maryse!" Her plump brown cheeks lift into a smile like I'm her favorite niece, and she stands to pull me into a hug, rubbing my back. "Aren't you a sight for sore eyes. Come sit now!"

"Hello, Auntie Ondine." I turn to the other one at the table, bowing my head respectful. "Auntie Margaret."

She glances up from doing stitchwork, a frown wrinkling her narrow face and dipping her bright pink hat. "Took you long enough to get here." She looks me up and down. "You put on weight?"

I grind my teeth behind my smile. Auntie Margaret is *that* kind of auntie.

"Oh, Maryse is just as she needs to be," Auntie Ondine insists, smoothing down the gold feathers crowning her purple hat. "Don't mind Auntie Margaret; she's a bit cranky today. Here, have some sweet tea."

She always a bit cranky, I think, accepting a mason jar. I stir the ice before sipping, a lemon wedge tickling my nose. Best sweet tea I ever tasted. Like somebody mixed up sugar and sunshine and goodness. Thing is, though, it ain't real. None of this is. Not the grass under my toes, this big shady oak tree, even the blue sky above. That stuff Molly was saying, about other worlds? This someplace like that, I think. Auntie Ondine say it look like this for my sake, to give me something familiar.

These three not people either. Never you mind they looking like aunties up in church on Sunday. They ain't got shadows, for one. Look just out the corner of your eye, their bodies start to shimmer and blur. One time I looked too long and all three changed. They was still womanlike, but slender and unsightly tall in long bloodred gowns. Their faces was masks stitched from what look like *real*

brown skin. What was beneath . . . well . . . reminded me
of foxes. With rusty fur, pointed ears, and burnt-orange
eyes. I know what it sounds like, Bruh Fox and all that. But
I saw what I saw!

I sip the sweet tea (that ain't really sweet tea) and turn to
the woman on the swing. "Hello, Auntie Jadine." She don't
answer. Just keeps swinging, a far-off look in her eyes.

"Oh, she's doing . . . her thing," Auntie Ondine apolo-
gizes.

That explains it, then. Auntie Jadine the strangest of these
three, and that's saying a lot. Time funny with her. She living
in the now, the yesterday, and tomorrow all at once. When
she like this, mean she's somewhere—*sometime*—else.

Nana Jean warns me to watch myself with these three.
Say haints is tricksy. But they remind me of my mama in a
way. Like they plucked memories of her from my head, and
made them into three people. Maybe that's why I'm fond
of them; remind me of what I lost. Besides, was them who
gave me the sword.

The broad black leaf-blade sits on the table, keeping a
steady hum that draws in spirits—their singing whispering in my ears.

Auntie Ondine told me how the sword came to be. The
one who made it, back in Africa he was a big to-do who
sold slaves, till he got tricked and sold too. Got made a
blacksmith, on account he was good with iron. He made
the sword to look like one that used to mark him as a big
to-do. Only bigger—not just for ceremony. He pounded it

with magic, calling on the dead who got sold away. He bid them sing their songs, seek the spirits of the ones who sent them across the sea, and bind those chiefs and kings, even his own self, up in that iron—make them serve those they done wrong.

When I call the sword I get visions from them angry slaves, their songs pulling at restless chiefs and kings bound to the blade, making them cry out until sleeping gods stir in answer. That's the sword's power—a thing of vengeance and repentance. Don't know how it ended up with these three. But they say it needs a champion. When it first came I wasn't no champion, though. Just a scared girl, hiding under the floorboards. But I learned how to listen since then—how to move to its rhythm.

"We apologize for calling on you at this late hour," Auntie Ondine says. "We tried to wait until you completed your physical intimacies with your beau."

Auntie Margaret humphs. "Lots of carrying on and grunting, you ask me."

My face goes warm. Not being people and all, these three sometimes say things they shouldn't. Like about my "physical intimacies." Or implying they was *watching* me! Someone laughs. I turn to find Auntie Jadine staring dead at me under her wide pale blue hat, that faraway look replaced by something devilish.

"When my man put it on me, he make my legs shake!" she bursts out.

I almost spit my sweet tea.

Did I mention Auntie Jadine only talks in song? Don't know where—or *when*—this one from. But the meaning clear enough. If I didn't have this wonderful sun-kissed skin, I'd be a perfect shade of scarlet.

Auntie Jadine grins, and I catch a hint of fox teeth. "He got dat good, good, good," she sings. "Dat good, good, good!" She jumps off the swing and walks over, yellow dress flowing across long black limbs as her bare feet tread grass. All three barefooted. Say shoes too hard to think up. She plants the softest kiss on my forehead before easing into a chair and taking up a jar of tea.

"In any case," Auntie Ondine continues. "We needed to talk. Ill tidings are afoot."

"The enemy is gathering," Auntie Margaret adds sharply.

The enemy what they call Ku Kluxes. Reason they gave me the sword was to fight them—their champion against that evil. Suddenly I remember my dream.

"And he say he the storm, this Butcher Clyde," I finish.

The three was quiet as I talked. Now they looking at me hard.

"Did this Butcher Clyde harm you in any way?" Auntie Ondine asks. "Give you anything to eat? Answer me!"

Her intensity surprises me. "Nothing— Wait, that really wasn't just a dream?"

"Not no dream!" Auntie Margaret snaps, jabbing a stitching needle at me. "You let the enemy in, girl!"

"What? I ain't let nobody—"

Auntie Ondine puts a soothing hand to mine, her doting

voice back. "You likely didn't mean to, baby. They find ways in, through some trouble you might keep deep down inside. Like leaving a door open. There something you can think of like that?"

I remember then the other dream. Back at my old house. The girl and her warning.

They like the places where we hurt.

"No," I answer, looking Auntie Ondine in the eye. Only way to tell a lie right.

"I know this lady who carry her troubles," Auntie Jadine sings in a bluesy voice. "Carry her troubles, all on her back. She gon' let them troubles weigh her down, she keep on carrying 'em round like that . . ."

I narrow my eyes at her, but she busy tracing a finger in her sweet tea.

"Well, we'll just have to be careful in the future." Auntie Ondine smiles.

"What's happening? Nana Jean can feel something too."

Auntie Ondine shakes her head. "We can't see. There's a . . . veil, and it's growing." She gestures to a patch of dark in the blue sky I hadn't noticed before. "Now this Butcher Clyde appears. An unlikely coincidence."

"None of it good," Auntie Margaret frets.

"You think this Butcher Clyde a Ku Klux?" I ask.

Auntie Ondine's face sours. "The enemy has more minions than we know."

I remember Molly's talk. "You mean ones that's smarter than Ku Kluxes?"

"Smarter and more dangerous. You must be careful now."

Her words eat up all the good feelings I'd held on to this night.

"Who are they? These Ku Kluxes and the ones minding them? *What* are they?"

Auntie Ondine looks like she's measuring what to tell me. Always seem like they *measuring*. I start to press again, but it's Auntie Margaret who talks.

"There were two brothers, Truth and Lie. One day they get to playing, throwing cutlasses up into the air. Them cutlasses come down and fast as can be—swish!—chop each of their faces clean off! Truth bend down, searching for his face. But with no eyes, he can't see. Lie, he sneaky. He snatch up Truth's face and run off! Zip! Now Lie go around wearing Truth's face, fooling everybody he meet." She stops stitching to fix me with stern eyes. "The enemy, they are the Lie. Plain and simple. The Lie running around pretending to be Truth."

I listen, wondering, *What's plain and simple about that?*

"Don't let their smile fool you," Auntie Jadine sings. "Or take you in."

"We should get you back," Auntie Ondine says. "Been here long already."

They strict about the time I spend in this place, though none at all will have passed back home. I grab my sword, getting another hug from Auntie Ondine.

"Be mindful what we tell you now. Stay clear of this Butcher Clyde."

"I will," I answer, certain to look her in her eyes.

As I walk away, I can hear Auntie Jadine at my back.

"When the devil come to town, you betta watch how you get down . . . watch, watch, watch out for the devil!"

FOUR

I'm near Cherry and Third in downtown Macon. People passing by glance to me. Probably because I'm back in knickers—blue with gold pinstripes tucked into gaiters and Oxfords. Or maybe because I'm whistling a tune named "La Madelon" Chef picked up in France. Mostly, though, it's the sword strapped to my back peeking over a cream-yellow shirt. Don't see that too often on a Thursday morning.

Butcher Clyde wasn't hard to find. His name in fresh red paint on yellow right over the shop across the street: Butcher Clyde's Choice Cuts & Grillery. The leaflet I'm holding announces the store's grand opening, offering free meats to patrons. Well, white patrons. Because the leaflet makes plain this here is a Klan establishment. It got a drawing of Uncle Sam hugging a man that resemble Butcher Clyde, both holding sausage links, reading: *Wholesome Food for the Moral White Family*.

Sure enough, there's four Klans in robes standing outside the store's glass window, directing the steady line of patrons. Two I know is Ku Kluxes, faces shifting as they pass a canteen back and forth.

I told Nana Jean about the dream with Butcher Clyde and my meeting with the Aunties. After she get through grumbling about haints, she admits he could be the "blood redhead buckrah man" from her premonitions. Seems he arrived in town a week back, opening up this shop next to the American National Bank building. She warned us to keep our distance. But a whole day gone, and I'm losing patience. This Butcher Clyde snuck into my head, outright threatened me. But I ain't no scared girl no more. I hunt monsters—they *don't* hunt me. So now I'm about to do something real brave or stupid.

I wait for a streetcar to pass, then cross Cherry Street, walking straight to Butcher Clyde's. White folk in line frown when I skip past them. Probably thinking I'm plumb out my mind when I march up to the Klans. One, a little bit of a man, looks at me like he gone dumb. I wait for him to recover.

"You lost, girl?"

"Nope," I respond. "Here to see Butcher Clyde. He know me."

White folk get thrown off if you act like they don't expect—least till they remember they gotta put you in your place. I play my other card, looking to a Ku Klux.

"I can see you." I tap under one eye. "Ugly as sin under that skin."

The green eyes of the man the Ku Klux wearing don't

blink. He stops drinking from the canteen, letting water run down his chin, and turns to the other Ku Klux, like they got a silent way of speaking. My gamble pays off.

"Let her through," the Ku Klux says.

The two human Klans set to holler, but I slip right in the door as someone leaves.

Bruh Rabbit walking into Bruh Gator's open jaws, my brother's voice whispers.

The inside look like any other butcher shop. Smells like one too—fresh blood and raw, open flesh. But there's also the scent of seared meat coming from a kitchen. And at tables, people sit eating. There's Klan posters everywhere, one advertising *The Birth of a Nation* at Stone Mountain Sunday. Men at the counter, every last one a Ku Klux, hand out brown packages to customers. And behind them is none other than Butcher Clyde.

He looks the same from the dream—a hefty bulk of a man. Like the other night he stands with his back to me, singing some awful tune and swinging his cleaver. I start up whistling, loud as I can, and he stops what he doing to turn slow. There's slight surprise when our eyes meet, but I don't stay for him to say nothing, walking to take a chair by the front window, leaning back all casual-like. A white lady and her son sitting nearby watch me open-mouthed. I stare back until she turns away. There's angry buzzing behind me, but Butcher Clyde cuts in.

"Brothers and sisters, don't let this disturb our feast. The lesser of God's creatures at times need to be guided righteously to recall their proper place. Rest assured, I will take this one in firm hand. Go on and eat now, eat! Fill up your bellies with the Lord's sustenance. Make the Invisible Empire strong!"

I don't bother to look while he making his speech, and I only turn when I hear him take the chair across from me. His red hair slick with pomade and he's wearing spectacles this time. There's patches of sweat all over him, soaking his underarms, and trickling down his shaved chin.

"You look hot. Must be cold, wherever you from."

He just grins and drawls, "Figured we'd see you soon, Maryse."

"I prefer you keep my name out your mouth, Clyde."

"Bold to come here alone. You know we're the only thing keeping you alive right now?" He leans forward, voice gone low. "One word and these good people would tear you limb from limb. Hang you from a light post."

I lean in to meet him, smiling. "What make you think I come alone, Clyde?"

I wonder if he can sense Sadie on a nearby rooftop, Winnie cocked and waiting. Or Chef in the old Packard, ready to toss a few homemade bombs through his window. Maybe he do, because he lets out a slow chuckle.

"Bold as brass." His eyes wander over my shoulder. "And with the sword."

"Want to see it up close?" I pull it from my back, slamming the blade flat on the table. The woman sitting near us squeaks, jumping up with her son and leaving.

Butcher Clyde don't flinch, his eyes tracing the triangular patterns cut into the black metal before returning to me. "No need for theatrics, Maryse. I'm sure you didn't wander in here just to make threats. You come because you have questions. Questions those three interlopers—your Aunties, is it?—won't tell. Ain't that right?" The answer on my face makes him break into a toothy grin. "Well, go on, then, ask us what you want to know. We tell you true."

Auntie Margaret hums in my ears. *They are the Lie.* But my lips already working.

"You a Ku Klux?"

He laughs. "Us? One of them? Like comparing you to a dog, which we understand they've developed a taste for. Not to worry, don't serve that here."

"A dog. So you they master, then?"

"*Master* might be a bit much. Think of us more like"—he twirls thick fingers, grabbing for a word—"management."

"Why you here?"

"Why, to fulfill the grand plan, of course."

"Which is?"

"Bringing the glory of our kind to your world. Putting an end to your strife and bickering. Relieving you of the abomination of your meaningless existence. We strive to give you purpose, which you will come to know once you have been properly joined to our harmonious union."

"Harmonious union?" I gesture at the Klan posters and whatnot. "That what you call this ode to the great white race?"

"Don't mind that. We need you to let us in, to merge you to our great collective." His gaze wanders over the shop's patrons. "They was just the most willing. So easy to devour from the inside, body and soul. Always have been."

A spike of anger hits me. "That why you have them go around killing us?"

"Oh, we might point them in a direction we need, but that hate they got in them is their own doing. You see, Maryse, we don't care about what skin you got or religion. Far as we concerned, you all just meat."

He rolls his neck, and as I watch sores break out across his skin—on his face, his forearms, his fingers. Not sores. Little mouths, like in the dream. Even his eyes roll back, leaving red gums and jagged teeth behind his spectacles. Every tongue flicks the air hungrily and right then, I see him. *Really* see him. Now I understand why he keeps saying *we* and *us*. This ain't one thing—it's dozens! I can see the places where they join together, stitched up in this human suit. They move about under his skin, like maggots in a corpse. A shiver shakes me and I grip my sword, imagining jumping up to slice that thick neck off his shoulders— and a hundred slithering things spilling out.

When he talks again, all those mouths talk too—dozens of shrill voices mashing together that only I can hear. "You haven't asked us the biggest question. Ask it. Ask it!"

I clench my teeth at the jarring chorus, but I ask, "What's coming?"

Those horrible mouths turn up into wicked grins.

"Grand Cyclops is coming," they croon. "When she do, your world is over."

I look at him, not understanding.

"We don't have to keep up this fight, Maryse. Told you we've been watching you. There's a special place for you in our grand plan."

"Fuck your grand plan," I spit back.

He laughs, and something deep in his belly growls.

"Such language! What would your mammy and pappy think?"

I almost put my sword through him right then and there.

"We apologize. Know that's a sore spot for you. Now see, we could use your fire. Really should hear us out. After all, you think your little ragtag friends and that witch— with her blue bottles and weak magic—can stand against us? That you going to stop what's coming with singing and Mama's Water? Look at your face! You think we don't know all about y'all? Girl, you even understand what you're fighting?"

He signals and I tense up. But the Ku Klux who steps forward don't even look at me. He just sets a plate on the table. I look down to see it's meat, cooked rare and bloody. It got a cut on the top—that suddenly opens up into a mouth and lets out a sharp *squeal!*

Take all I got not to flip that table over as the meat begins inching its way across my plate. I turn to look about the shop, where people are eating. Devouring this living meat. Shoving it in they mouths like hogs at slop, chewing and grinding and swallowing it into their bellies. The sight brings up bile in my throat. I snatch a fork and stab the meat, holding it down while it screech and wriggle.

"One day," I growl, "I'm going to cut you up into little pieces."

I snatch my sword, lifting up and pushing from the table. The Ku Kluxes stare at me, intent in their eyes. But Butcher Clyde gives the slightest shake of his head. I look out at the people, transfixed in their eating, and turn away quick, wanting to be out of this place. A multitude of voices catch me as I reach the door. "Good of you to come by. Of course you know, this means we have to return the favor. Be seeing you, real soon." Laughter from a hundred mouths chase me from the shop, a jarring chorus of razors in my ears.

"Don't know why we can't just play Spades," Sadie grumbles. She's sitting slouched in her too-big overalls, Winnie at her side. "And how you learn a Kraut game anyway? Y'all gone over there to kill 'em or play cards with 'em?"

Chef flashes that easy smile, shuffling the deck as the slim cards blur between her fingers. We at Nana Jean's. The farmhouse full with people and the kerosene lamps flicker our shadows big off the walls. I check my new pocket watch, brass instead of silver. Half past eleven. The hour late.

"Picked it up from some German soldiers we caught,"

Chef answers. "None of 'em coulda been older than sixteen. White boys told them Negroes had tails and we was cannibals. So the Germans we captured was extra friendly, thinking teaching us card games would stop them from getting eaten." She pulls the smoking Chesterfield from her lips to flick ashes, before her face goes dark. "Then we come up on a Kraut patrol and one of them tries to give away our position. Had to slit his throat myself. Stupid kid."

"You have any *good* stories 'bout that war?" Sadie asks.

Emma Krauss pulls up a chair, face bright as she spreads out her prim brown dress and lays the shotgun she carrying in her lap—what she calls a Merkel. Thing look bigger than she do. "Meine Freundin Cordelia. Deal me in. My sisters played this game. Though, I am not very good."

Chef lifts an eyebrow. "Since when are revolutionaries into bourgeois pastimes?"

"On the contrary, I am quite fond of cards! Games of skill and chance, that place every man and woman on a level field."

"Unless the one dealing stacks the deck against you," Chef counters.

Emma peers down her spectacles. "Why, Cordelia, you sound like a socialist."

Chef whoops a laugh, dealing the widow in.

"Y'all want me to keep playing, I don't want none of that talk," Sadie warns. "Bad enough I gotta spend Saturday night cooped up in here." Her face softens into a lopsided smile. "You know who got the best conversations? That Lester. He know the most amazing things. Going on about old rulers of Ethiopia. You know he say there was this place named Meroe ruled by queens? You imagine that? Colored women ruling? Bet I woulda made a fine queen of Meroe. Strutting around on elephants or whatever."

"I believe Meroe is old Nubia," Emma adds. "One of their kings saved Israel from the Assyrians."

"See there! I bet Lester know about that. Can listen to him all day!"

"So you been telling us," Chef murmurs. "Suppose that Lester done some mighty fine talking the other night."

Sadie narrows her eyes. "You got a sinful mind, Cordelia Lawrence."

Chef winks my way. "You want in?"

Not sure she mean the game or ribbing Sadie. I shake my head. Used to pester my brother to teach me cards like he played secret with his friends. He taught me my letters, figuring, even how to fish. But never got around to cards. I fold up my book, walking off.

When I told Nana Jean about my meeting with Butcher Clyde she was hotter than fish grease. Say I was a fool gone wandering into a wolf's den. I tried to make her see we need to know what them Ku Kluxes is planning. She stays mad, but agree with me about the meaning of Butcher Clyde's parting words. He coming after us. And we been getting ready since.

I pass by where the Shouters sit, holding hands while

Uncle Will leads a prayer. Nana Jean convinced them it too dangerous to set out on the road with Ku Kluxes about. If Butcher Clyde know as much as he say, sure he know about them. *We been watching you a long time, Maryse.* I shake off his words, reaching to where the Gullah woman sits in her chair. Molly there with her, reading over coded resistance telegraphs.

"There's Ku Klux activity all through the state," she's saying. "Mrs. Wells-Barnett's operatives report Klans gathering at Stone Mountain, for that movie."

"The Grand Cyclops." Both turn to look at me. "Butcher Clyde, he say whatever coming is big. Stone Mountain where they did the conjuring what started all this. Has to be where this Grand Cyclops coming!"

"Bet the government know 'bout it too!" Sadie yells out. We ignore her.

"Indians used to meet there," Molly says thoughtfully. "The mountain might be a focal point where worlds meet too. Makes sense why Simmons used it to open his door. Maybe planning to do it again, to bring this . . . Cyclops."

Nana Jean frowns when she looks at me, bushy eyebrows bristling. Still mad, then. "De haint ooman dem ain say nuttin?"

I shake my head. Thought Auntie Ondine would have summoned me by now, but haven't heard a word. "We need to let people know what's set to happen on Stone Mountain. Tell them we have to stop it."

"From what's coming across the wires, could be Klan

there in the hundreds," Molly says. "Who knows how many are turned."

"Then we get who we can. We need to be there!"

"Ki! How we gwine git dey when we yuh?" Nana Jean huffs.

"She's right," Molly agrees. "Don't look at me like that. I'm not casting blame. But we've been holed up here expecting an attack. Can't be in two places at once."

They right I know. Since Butcher Clyde made his threat, we been trapped here. Stayed up all last night, and the night before that, but nothing. Now here it is Saturday almost heading into Sunday morning. And still quiet. Doubt starts creeping in. Maybe Butcher Clyde aiming to throw me off. Keep us out the way while he go about doing his evil.

A sharp rap on the door sends me whirling, ready to call my sword. I ain't the only one. Chef standing up with her knife. Emma holding her shotgun and Sadie somehow already got a bullet in the chamber, looking down the sights of her Winchester. But then the rap comes twice again, and once more.

Molly jumps up. "One of mine!"

She reaches the door and pulls it open. Sure enough it's one of her apprentices with a rifle slung over her shoulder. Molly says she's terrible with guns, but at least two of the young Choctaw women she teaching nice with the weapons. This one got on a wide-brimmed black hat. Sethe, I think, and she's holding someone small by the back of the neck. One of the boys who helps pack up Mama's Water.

"Klans!" he pants, small chest heaving. "My papa make me run all the way here. Tell you, Klans attacking!"

"Where?" I ask, pushing forward.

He takes another gulp of air. "Frenchy's!"

Notation 21:

In This Field We Must Die? Well, that Shout got many meanings. The field where the slaves was forced to toil away they whole lives. Or it's this world everybody got to leave one day. What else there was to do in that drudgery, working from can't see morning to can't see night, but to get to thinking on life, death, and God's purpose? All them grand thinkers lost to the whip. Gone and took they secrets with 'em to the grave.

—Interview with Ms. Henrietta Davis, age seventy-two, transliterated from the Gullah by EK

FIVE

The old Packard races down Macon's country roads, engine rattling noisily in the night. Beside me Sadie chewing on tobacco so hard I can hear her teeth snapping. For once I hold back telling her to stop smacking in my ear. She worried I know. We all is.

Was all confusion when we get the news. Attack shoulda been on us, not Frenchy's. For a while there was just a mess of arguing and shouting. Sadie the one who finally grabbed her rifle and headed for the door, saying she don't got time to sit around fussing. Me and Chef joined her, leaving Molly's people and Emma to guard Nana Jean's. All our fears get made real when we catch sight of what's in the distance.

Frenchy's on fire, orange flames bright against the night. People run past us on the road, still in their fine clothes. Saturday night the juke joint would be packed. Worst time for this to happen. I search their faces, belly in knots as I look for Michael George. I know better, though. He wouldn't leave the place he built and set down roots.

Chef finally has to stop the Packard, unable to drive

through the fleeing people. We jump out, pushing through them. Klans, they saying—came in tearing up the place, whipping people. One man show his shirt torn to shreds, his back bloody. Another one wild-eyed, raving about monsters. Ku Kluxes. The sight can come on you like that. When we finally reach Frenchy's, we can see the mayhem ourselves.

The juke joint hardly look the same. The whole porch blackened, and flames licking the second floor. People running through the front, stumbling and falling to get out. And right there waiting is a whole mess of Klans. All in white robes, with hoods over their heads so you can only make out eyes. But I can still tell which is Ku Kluxes. And there's no mistaking the big one at their head, holding up a Bible and shouting.

Butcher Clyde.

"Brethren, we must do our best to stamp out the vices in our midst! Fornication! Drinking! Heathen music! It's left to us to correct the waywardness of these simple minds, as a father must govern over his children and home—delivering stripes onto the wicked so that they might be persuaded to follow a straight path!"

People fleeing the fire forced to run through the mob, and Klans with whips strike whoever they can. The sound of the lash biting flesh sets my blood boiling. I start forward, but Chef grabs hold of me, pointing at the burning juke joint.

"There's people still in there!"

I look to a window to see the shadows of men and women trapped in the blaze. They run out of sight, and a set of bigger shadows lumber after them. Ku Kluxes!

Sadie growls, taking off running to the back of the house. Don't have much choice but to follow. We reach a door to find it braced with a bar—to make folk run through the front. Or burn up inside. Soon as we pull it away, people come flying out, coughing and doubling over. We let them pass, then run in.

Flames and smoke greet us, but through the haze I spot the first Ku Klux—a full turned demon amid hellfire. It got an arm ready to slash at some people cornered against a wall. I don't wait to figure out more.

The sword comes at my call, with the visions. A woman in Saint-Domingue shouting a war song at shaken French troops as she set herself on fire; a man in Cuba applying a balm to another's cut-open back, singing to soothe his lover's cries; a mother fleeing through thick Mississippi pines to a contraband camp, humming to quiet her babies. The girl in the dark there too, and I shrug off her fear before it can sink in teeth.

The sword grows solid in my grip, black smoke becoming metal as I run the blade through the Ku Klux's back, right where one of its hearts is. Thank goodness for Molly's dissections. It staggers, falling onto its side, and I drive my sword into its throat. The people I saved stand there bug-eyed. If they ain't got the sight, they just seen me put several inches of iron through a man's neck.

"We try to fight him," one stutters. "But he strong like . . . ain't natural!"

"Y'all move! Get on out—"

I don't finish before something crashes into me. I land on my back and the air rushes out my lungs. When I suck some back in, the smoke sets me to choking. Between tears, I can see a Ku Klux on top of me. Where the blazes this one come from? Its jaws are clamped down and there's a hot trickle on me. This thing biting my arm off? No, my sword. And the wetness is its saliva. Disgusting.

With all the strength I can muster, I call on the sword's power. Those old man-stealing kings and chiefs wail the names of sleeping gods, and the black leaf-blade turns white hot in the Ku Klux's mouth. It shrieks, scrambling off me and clawing its face, most of which is charred meat now. I move to finish it off, but a bullet takes it in the flank. The cornered people ain't moved, and now they're screaming. They scream harder when a second bullet pierces the Ku Klux's eyes, dropping it dead.

I look to find Sadie, aiming Winnie right at me. "What—?"

"Drop down!"

I got sense enough to go back flat. A bullet zips overhead and there's another shriek. I whip my head around to see two Ku Kluxes wrapped in fire, charging on all fours from another room. Sadie works that lever and shoots so fast, I barely have time to count before it's over—one bullet, three, five. Now there's two more dead Ku Kluxes.

The cornered people stop screaming. At least two fainted. Maybe the rest gone hoarse. But they ain't moving neither, just hugging the wall and shaking. Chef appears, coaxing them away. "Help me get these outside!" she shouts between coughs, lifting a limp man. "This whole place going to burn down!"

I start to grab a woman when a set of screams come. We all look up. The second floor. Michael George?

"I'll go!" I say.

"By yo'self?" Sadie shouts.

But I'm already moving.

Running up the stairs feels like I'm heading into the belly of some fire-breathing dragon. It's hotter here and the smoke almost blinding. I follow the screams down a corridor to where a Ku Klux is throwing itself against a door. On the other side, the screams come every time it hits. I give a shrill whistle, and the monster swings a six-eyed head my way. Roaring, it comes for me, and I run straight for it, dropping to my knees and letting momentum carry me across the floor to slice through its underside. It passes me, stumbles out of its run, and whips back around, slipping and falling forward on its spilled entrails. At the door, the screams come again. I shout at them to open it and have to cuss before they do. Not Michael George. A trembling man and woman, clothes half off. No need to wonder what they was up to.

"You need to get out!" I tell them.

We have to clear back the barricade they erected—a

bed and chifforobe. Soon as I get them into the hall, they see the dying Ku Klux crawling after me in its mess and start hollering. Rolling my eyes, I reach to put my sword through the monster's skull. That makes them holler more. I'm telling them to do less crying and more moving when there's the sound of breaking glass followed by a crash. It comes several more times. Then there's heavy thudding like galloping and—

The doors to one of the rooms splinters open to show three Ku Kluxes fighting their way through the narrow space. More doors bust open, and more Ku Kluxes follow. The damn things climbed up the house and are coming through the top windows! The corridor fills with them, in front and behind. I stop counting at eight. The way they all turn my way, eyes glittering, easy to figure out who they here for. I raise my sword and let it sing.

The next moments are a whirlwind—snapping teeth, claws, and blood, plus two people screaming behind me. It don't make for pretty fighting. I cut wide arcs, trying best I can to keep the monsters back. But soon as I make space, more crowd in. Can't keep this up. Between my lungs choking with smoke and the heat of the fire, I'm fading fast. A Ku Klux almost slices me open before I spin to bat it back. I'm starting to wonder if there's no way out this mess when there's a shout and the blessed sound of a Winchester loading. Sadie's at the edge of the stairs, looking like a yella angel in overalls come down to fight in hell. Her face lit fierce by flames as she holds up Winnie like a sword of judgment.

In a blur she shoots down Ku Kluxes not in front of her but behind me! The shots are straight for the head. Dropping two with one bullet. I never seen anything like it. Before you can even count to four, the path behind me is clear.

"Go!" she yells.

I take steps to help her, thinking of the two of us back to back, taking on this whole bunch. But she waves her rifle at me and yells again.

"Stop being hardheaded just this once! Take them and I'll follow behind!"

Right, then. I take hold of the dazed couple, pushing them on. As we run I hear Sadie shouting, "Listen up, all you white niggers! Just you and me and Winnie now!" A set of angry roars answer, and I glance back to see every last Ku Klux surging toward her in a pack of pale skin, venting their rage. In between the smoke I catch Sadie laughing as they come, working the lever of her Winchester and firing like there's no tomorrow.

Rifle shots ring in my ears as we reach the back stairway. We run, stumble, almost fall a few times through the thick haze. When we reach the door, we stagger out, gulping night air. I'm bent over hacking my lungs out when Chef runs up. She with a familiar face—Lester. Got a cut on his forehead, but otherwise look well.

"Michael George!" I cough. "You seen him?"

A pained look cross his face. "Them Klans take him!"

I glance up sharp. "How you mean?"

"People tell me the same," Chef says. "That the Klans was snatching folk. Maybe a half dozen. Packed them into cars and drove off."

I picture Michael George, fighting as they drag him away. But why would they take him or anyone else? Don't make sense!

"Sadie," Lester says, face frantic. "Where's Sadie?"

I'm set to tell him she right behind me but when I look back, nobody there. And I realize it been a while since I heard a rifle shot. My eyes go to the burning juke joint and my stomach drops. I take off in a run, ignoring Chef's calls and, taking one big swallow of good air, dive back into the smoke and fire.

Can barely make out anything now, and I trip and bounce off a wall before finding the back stairs. The smoke got my eyes streaming tears and my lungs burning. But I can't stop. When I reach the top and turn into the corridor I stare at the scene before me.

There's dead Ku Kluxes everywhere. Most turning to ash, but the fire catches some and the stink of their unnatural flesh scalds my nostrils. I cover my mouth and nose with my cap, blocking out the smoke and stench best I can, clambering over bodies. Must be about a dozen lining the floor—but no Sadie. I shout, not getting an answer, and for a brief moment I imagine she got out some other way. Then at the end of the corridor I spy the woodgrain of a rifle butt. Fear eats up my hope. When I reach, it takes all my strength to push the Ku Klux lying atop the rifle away.

Underneath is Sadie.

She sits propped against a wall. And she's . . . I swallow. Lord, she tore up bad.

Her overalls shredded, and the checkered shirt soaked in blood. The arm holding Winnie is a ruin of open flesh and she got her other hand pressed to her middle. When I grip her shoulder, calling her name, big brown eyes open to fix on me. Her lips gone pale, and she works to mumble. "Maryse. Why you yelling and making all that noise?"

Hadn't noticed I was yelling.

"You see all them Ku Kluxes me and Winnie got?"

"I see them. Can you stand? We gotta get out!"

She chokes on a laugh. "Stand? Don't know if I still got legs. They gone numb. Can't feel my hands much neither. And it's shivering cold."

"I'll carry you! Can't weigh more than some change."

The corner of her mouth rises at my joke, but then she lets out a haggard breath. "Don't think I'm leaving Frenchy's tonight." She lifts the hand from her middle and I choke on a gasp. Her belly been ripped clean open, pouring blood. I press my cap against the wound, trying to make it stop. Please, God, make it stop!

Sadie pushes feebly at my hand. "You need to go, Maryse. No sense we both burn up in here. You just make sure they give me a nice funeral."

"No!" I shout, coughing on smoke. "Plan your own damn funeral!"

But she keep talking like she don't hear me. "Up in a church. I know I ain't go much, but I want one anyhow. With a big choir too. And lots of singing. Make sure Lester up front, bawling his eyes out. Tell him I don't want him to move on just yet. He should pine over me so that it mess up anything he try to have with the next two or three women who come along. And you and Chef do something special for me. Something you know I'd like."

"Sadie . . . ," I whimper.

Her eyes turn to me. "My grandpappy say when we die, we get our wings back, the ones white folk cut off when we come here. Maybe I'll fly and meet my mama. Or all the way back to Africy. Lester tell me one of those queens of Meroe fought them Romans. She was a mean lady too, with an eyepatch. Cut the head off one their statues and buried it under her palace! Ain't that something? I woulda made a damn good queen! Can you picture me with an eyepatch, Maryse?"

I don't get to answer. Because Sadie dies right there in my arms.

Laying her still body back against the wall, I smooth her hair, letting her braid fall in the front the way she like. Then I put her arms around Winnie, before kissing her forehead and saying goodbye.

When I leave, it ain't through the back. I head down what's left of the main stairs, the smoke and flames no longer bothering me. There's a heat building in me far worse. When I hit the floor I start up into a run. Think part of my clothes is on fire but don't much care. I aim for the front door, launching out into the night,

The first Klan who looks up stares wild-eyed behind his hood as I fly through the air, screaming like a banshee. I'm set to bury my humming blade right through his skull, but he not a Ku Klux—just a man. And I gave my word to Nana Jean. So I cut off his hand instead. He stares dumb as it flies away with the whip and I kick him in the chest to send him sprawling. Another Klan I hamstring, listening to his screams as he drops. A third I smack in the face with the flat of my wide blade once, twice, till I hear the satisfied crunch of breaking teeth as blood stains his white hood. But they not who I want. The rage in me needs to kill something. Something that ain't people.

Several Ku Kluxes finally appear. I scream at them to change. I want to murder them as monsters. But they fall back. The Klans too. Finally one steps up, big and broad. Butcher Clyde.

"Maryse," he calls. "Told you we'd see each other again soon."

"I'm going to kill you," I tell him plain.

"Why, Maryse, we don't think we've seen you so mad." The eyes behind that hood read me. "Mmm, there's loss there. Something unfortunate happen to one of your friends. The tall one? No? Ohhh! The one like spitfire! With the rifle! Sweet little Sadie?"

I'm on him soon as her name drops out his foul mouth. In my head the spirits of vengeful slaves cry out, and I feel their anger in my swing, eager to take his head off. But he pulls back, faster than I'd expected, and my sword meets metal with a sharp clang that reverberates up my arm. A cleaver. I come at him again, only to be met by another cleaver. He uses both as I hammer at him, blocking me at every turn.

Frustrated, I pull back, catching my breath. He chuckles.

"Told you already, we're no dog to be put down. You a might better with that little trinket, give you that. Better than that night outside Memphis."

His words send me stiff. And under that hood, I imagine he grins. "Really think we didn't know where you was hiding? Beneath the floorboards, in the dark, shivering and shaking. Of course we did. But we needed you to become who you are now. Needed to fill you up with horror. Anger. Why we left you that little present in the barn."

Something in me breaks. I snarl like I ain't human no more, white-hot fury behind my swings that strike sparks off his cleavers. I don't want to just kill him, I want to end him utterly so that nothing's left. The song in my ears is blaring, pounding with my blood. For a moment I'm sure I have him, until he starts to sing.

It don't come from his mouth, not the one on his face. It's those other mouths, the small ones all opening now under his robes, singing in a chorus without harmony or pattern. Like in the dream, it hurts. A sharpness that cuts through me, distorting my rhythm. I stagger off beat, my song fluttering in my grasp like a thread. I try to catch it, but it slips away—gone.

I stumble as Butcher Clyde's song pours into my ears. My swings go wrong. I can't even keep my balance, tripping on my own feet, slipping to one knee and bringing my sword up as two cleavers descend in a silver flash. There's a jolt as they hit, sending pain through my body. As I watch, stunned, my blade seems to warp with this awful singing, turning brittle—before it shatters.

My mind won't accept what just happened, even as the broken sword pelts me with metal that turns to smoke and my hand goes empty. I call out for the blade, for the songs and the visions. But there's only Butcher Clyde's terrible disharmony filling the emptiness. He places the cleaver's edge right under my chin, forcing me to look into eyes turned to mouths studded with teeth.

"No other way this could end," those mouths speak at once. "Hate is *our* domain. Those meddling Aunties never told you why you were chosen to wield that sword? Just filled your head with stories about being their champion? Think what you will of us—at least we tell you true. Said before we wanted to make an offer, Maryse. Give you what you want more than anything—power over life and death."

"Go to hell!" I spit. "You got nothing I want!"

He shakes his head, pulling off his hood. "Perhaps you need to be made more amenable." He sticks out a fleshy tongue to pinch off a piece that squirms between his fingers. Behind me a Ku Klux grips my head, prying my jaws apart. I watch that unnatural meat come close, wriggling and reaching for my lips, eager to push its way inside. For some reason, only thing I can think of is my brother telling me 'bout Bruh Rabbit, caught and trying to trick Bruh Fox into letting him go.

Gon' ahead and roast me or skin me—just don't throw me in that briar patch!

A shrill whistle goes up. Butcher Clyde turns, and I follow to what he's looking at. Chef! She holding a stick of dynamite in one hand and her lighter in the other.

"I don't know what the fuck you are," she says. "But Imma need you to let her go, or I might have to do something drastic. Got enough blasting powder and silver enough to blow all your ugly asses to kingdom come. Best believe that."

Butcher Clyde eyes her before giving a signal. The hands holding me let go and I get up, staggering over to Chef, who catches me. Together we back off a ways before she bends down to whisper, "I don't have any more dynamite! Or silver! Run!"

We do. I turn back once to see if we being chased. But the Klans and Ku Kluxes just standing there. My eyes meet Butcher Clyde's.

"Come see us, Maryse!" he calls. "You know where! Told you, we got what you want! More than anything!"

SIX

Nana Jean's farmhouse feels like a tomb. Been an hour since we got back. The Gullah woman took the news hard. She in her chair, a hand covering her face while Molly tries to console her. Chef over at a table holding hands with Emma. The rest of the Shouters are singing some mournful song as the Stick Man beats a slow funeral march.

> *I walk in de moonlight, I walk in de starlight,*
> *To lay dis body down.*
> *I'll walk in de graveyard, I'll walk through the graveyard,*
> *To lay dis body down.*

Their voices sound a deep wailing, filling up the place with its strength. But none of it feels real.

Sadie. Dead. How can that be real?

Was just hours ago we was here, listening to her complain and carry on. Now she's gone—burned up inside a juke joint. My fists clench as I pace about, digging nails into my palms until it hurts. That pain at least feels real.

"What we gon' do?" I call out, needing to talk. Either that or I'll scream.

All eyes turn to me. Even the Shouters go quiet.

"Do about what?" Molly finally asks.

I stare like she lost her mind. "Them Ku Kluxes is still meeting to do their conjuring! This Grand Cyclops still coming!"

"Not sure what we can do for it," Molly answers. "The numbers against us—"

"Then get word to Atlanta to send whoever can come!"

She look skeptical and I think to Michael George.

"What about the people they took?"

"Likely for this ritual," Emma puts in. "They have spilled blood for such before."

"We just gon' let them stay taken?" I ask.

Molly frowns. "We could walk into a trap."

"Cordelia says you've lost your sword?" Emma asks. At this, Molly's eyebrows rise and Nana Jean looks up sharp. I glare at Chef, but she keeps her head down. "With the terrible loss of Sadie, our forces are stretched thin."

I shake my head. "We'll find a way. Chef. You could rig up some bombs, blow them right off that mountain!"

"Fool buckrah dem too?" Nana Jean asks.

"And women and children," Molly adds. "They invite them to rituals now."

"All of them! I don't care if they people or monsters! Blow up every last one! Make them pay for what they done!" I don't realize I'm shouting till the room goes quiet again, and the whoosh of pounding blood fills my ears.

"That not going to bring her back," Chef whispers. She looks up at me, eyes red and wet. I fight to talk, but it's like the anger gripping my tongue.

"Hunnah bex down," Nana Jean tells me. "Gwine bun up."

She right. My skin on fire. Feel like I could rip it off. I turn and stalk through the front door. Chef calls out but I'm already off the porch, making my way into the yard of bottle trees. There's a hornet's nest in my head I can't get quiet—as if a piece of Butcher Clyde's awful singing wormed its way inside. Even worse is the guilt gnawing my insides. Whispering that I stirred all this up. That Sadie's death is my fault. Looking to the night sky, I let out that scream I been holding in and start shouting.

"Where you at? Give me the sword and now take it back? Leave me with nothing?" Molly's apprentices stand guard on the porch, eyeing me. But I don't care. "If I'm your champion, then help me! Tell me what I have to do! Damn you, answer me!"

In anger I kick at one of the bottle trees and go tumbling, falling to land on my backside—somewhere else.

I scramble up on unsteady feet, swaying from the dizziness. The blue sky without a sun is now an angry orange with bits of lightning dancing across it. The big oak ain't got leaves no more and long black sheets hang from bare branches, blowing in a breeze I can't feel. Auntie Ondine, Auntie Margaret, and Auntie Jadine all there, wearing black dresses and broad black hats. A dark table sits between them. No drink or food this time, just a bundle of black cloth.

"Did you know?" I shout at Auntie Jadine. "You see what coming! Did you—?"

She runs forward, embracing me. I fight her, but she holds me tight, singing the same mourning song the Shouters was:

I'll lie in de grave and stretch out my arms,
Lay dis body down.
And my soul and your soul will meet in de day,
When I lay dis body down.

I don't know why, but those words from her lips send every feeling I been keeping back this night pouring out. I fall into her, loosing a cry filled with a pain I ain't tried to feel in seven years. Since the night I lost . . .

I lay there sobbing until I can catch a breath, then look up to face them.

"I needed you and you wasn't there."

Auntie Ondine glances to the angry sky. "The veil . . . has grown."

"The enemy cut us off from your world!" Auntie Margaret grumbles.

"Then how did I get here?"

"You wanted to very badly," Auntie Ondine says. "Sometimes that is enough."

Then I remember. "My sword, it—"

Auntie Ondine's face falls and they all look to the bundle on the table. I disentangle from Auntie Jadine, walking up to find my sword, nestled in black cloth. The dark leaf-blade is in pieces, a jagged edge jutting from the silver hilt. I run fingers along the fragments. There's no song. No nothing.

"It returned when broken," Auntie Ondine explains.

"Can you fix it?"

Auntie Margaret sucks her teeth. "Nobody can do that but you."

As usual, I got no idea what that means. But there's other things need discussing. I tell them about my confrontations with Butcher Clyde, about what he says is coming.

"There's an evil going on," Auntie Jadine hums darkly.

"This Grand Cyclops." Auntie Ondine's mouth twists up at the name. "It is an incarnation of the enemy, given flesh. I fear what it means for your world."

"It gon' mean the end!" Auntie Margaret huffs.

"Butcher Clyde, he tell more than that. He say he and the Ku Kluxes came looking for me seven years back. That they the ones who . . ." I can't say the rest.

All three exchange looks before Auntie Ondine nods slow.

Her answer hits like a hammer. "So all that they done, was because they wanted me? Why did you choose me as your champion?"

More exchanged glances, and I fight not to start shouting.

"To stop you from being theirs," Auntie Ondine says finally.

I step back, staggered. "That don't make sense!"

"They didn't come to kill you that night," Auntie Ondine says. "Not in body."

"Enemy have a prophecy," Auntie Margaret says. "To steal our champion. Make her over as theirs."

"We stopped them from taking you," Auntie Ondine explains. "To undo their plans. But I fear we may have unwittingly done their bidding." She looks to the broken sword. "The weapon is a thing of vengeance. The wielder must pour their own anger and suffering into it. We thought it could take away your pain. But we have only fed that wound, made you into a killer."

"It's a sword," I snap. "What else could I be?"

Auntie Ondine eyes me stern. "Very soon, the enemy will make an offer. How you choose will determine the fate of your world."

I glare back, set to tell her she crazy, until I remember Butcher Clyde's words: *Said before we wanted to make an offer, Maryse. Give you what you want more than anything—power over life and death.* I shake my head. "What they got to offer to make me side with them? They kill my people! People who look like me!"

"We can't see—the enemy veils it from us . . ." Auntie Ondine begins.

"But you done accepted it more than once already," Auntie Margaret finishes.

I don't even have the words to ask at what she means.

"You know that Auntie Jadine can perceive the now, yesterday, and tomorrow," Auntie Ondine says. "But it's more than that. She can perceive *many* tomorrows."

Now they really talking crazy. "How can there be more than one tomorrow?"

Auntie Margaret sighs. "Girl, every choice we make is a new tomorrow. Whole worlds waiting to be born."

"In some, you accept the enemy's offer, and all is darkness," Auntie Ondine says. "Always at this point—the tip of the sword on which your world balances."

I look at Auntie Jadine. What could those things living under Butcher Clyde's skin offer me to make me betray all I care about?

Power over life and death.

"And if I don't accept this offer, then we win? No more Ku Kluxes?"

"If you don't accept," Auntie Ondine answers, "there is the chance to continue the struggle. The hope at one day seeing victory. No more."

That don't seem fair.

I got a hundred questions but there's more pressing things at hand. "We need to stop this Grand Cyclops. Not enough of us, though. We need help. Your help. With you all there, we could—"

But Auntie Ondine already shaking her head, a face full

of sorry. "We made a choice long ago, to be bound to this place. Should we leave it, our powers would be lost. We may not even survive the crossing. You will have to face this on your own."

"But we just people!" I shoot back. "They're monsters! We need—"

"You need monsters," Auntie Margaret murmurs, eyes squinting up in thought.

Auntie Ondine turns to her. "What are you saying?"

"That there are others who might yet intervene."

"What others? Most don't visit their world and take no interest in them."

"I can think of some who do."

"Doctor, Doctor," Auntie Jadine sings. "Can you heal my loving pain . . ."

Auntie Ondine's head whips around. Her lips peel back, and I catch glimpses of sharp fox teeth. "No! Not them. There is no *love* in them. Leeches! Dead things, unfeeling with cold, desiccated hearts—seeking sustenance in misery!"

Auntie Jadine shrugs. "Can't blame a monster for doing what he do."

"They are amoral, chaotic!" Auntie Ondine insists. "With no care for our war!"

"Maybe." Auntie Margaret nods. "But they might find the enemy to their . . . taste?"

Auntie Jadine grins wide. Oh yes, definitely fox teeth.

Auntie Ondine's face goes thoughtful. Finally she looks

to me. "My sisters believe there are others who might ally with you against the enemy. You would have to convince them. But be warned. They will exact a price."

What's one more debt on top of all I got? "Who are they?"

"Their true names are lost," Auntie Ondine says. "But they have been to your world before." She lifts a hand, wriggling her fingers like she writing in the air. "There. You will find what you need in your book."

My book? I put a hand to my back pocket. Sure enough, my book is there. I take it out and flip through pages, wondering if they mean me to find stories of the breath stealer Boo Hag or poor Big Liz, the headless slave girl. But then I stop. There's a story that wasn't here before.

I frown at the title. "What are *Night Doctors*?"

"New players on the board perhaps," Auntie Ondine murmurs, tapping her chin.

"Playa, playa," Auntie Jadine hums devilishly, a bit of tongue peeking between foxy teeth.

Nana Jean's face frowns deep as I recount my meeting with the Aunties. She stay quiet, just sits in her chair staring at nothing. It's Chef who speaks.

Night Doctors, Night Doctors
Sneak in under your door.
Thief a nigger tongue and eyes
Then come back for more.

Night Doctors, Night Doctors,
Take you live or dead,
Snip off a nigger's hands and feet,
And even take his head.

Night Doctors, Night Doctors,
Snatch you to they white hall.
Cut a poor nigger child wide open,
Show him his liver and his gall

Night Doctors, Night Doctors
You can cry and carry on.
But when they done dissectin'
Every bit of you is gone.

When she finishes, the farmhouse is still. Outside the wind whistles through the bottle trees, the trapped haints either laughing wicked or wailing with fright. The Shouters take to staring at me like I'm John the Conqueror run off with the devil's daughter.

"Who are these Night Doctors?" Emma asks, looking around for answers.

Across the table Chef leans back, a joker between her fingers. "Stories. Heard it from a fella in my unit, whose people was from Virginia. Told us about his great-grandpappy's talk from slavery times. Night Doctors was supposed to be haints—tall and dressed in white—who stole away slaves and experimented on them. But none of its real. Was just old masters going around at night scaring slaves. Hear it came about, on account they sold the bodies of dead slaves to medical schools to cut up."

Emma gasps. "That's ghastly!"

Chef shrugs. "All of it was. But like I say, just old stories. No such thing as Night Doctors. They not real." Her eyes turn to me, then Nana Jean. "They not real, right?"

The Gullah woman twists up her lips. "Night Doctors, dem ain a story. Disya tale true." Her brown-gold gaze bores into me. "Hunnuh fuh go ta de ebil place t'night?"

I nod. "Need all the help we can get. I ain't asking permission." I try to sound defiant, but feel more like a little girl sassing off.

"Haint ooman dem tell hunnuh de way?"

I lift up my book of folktales. "Everything I need in here."

"Ain hab no sode 'do."

"It broke," is all I manage.

Old woman never liked that blade, but her face now say she don't like me going off without it neither. Still, she gives a nod—not permission, but at least understanding. Don't realize how much I want that, till she done it.

"Mine yo self," she warns low. "Dat ebil place ain like yuh. Hunnuh don' tek cyare hunnuh git turn 'bout een dey hall. Wensoneba people dem da gwine dey, dey da gii up sump'n. Leabe sump'n b'hin. Sway hunnuh gwine come back yuh whole?"

"Whole as I can," I say, remembering I don't make promises.

Notation 25:

The Shout *Eve and Adam* tell 'bout them two listening to that wicked snake and eating the fruit from the forbidden tree. When God call out, Adam don't answer. So He get to asking Eve. She say Adam going 'round picking up leaves to hide his nakedness, now that he know shame. When we do that Shout, we go 'round pretending to gather up leaves like Adam, hiding from the Lord. Suppose we making fun but it's a warning too—be mindful of getting mixed up with old wicked snakes.

—Interview with Ms. Susyanna "Susy" Woodberry, age sixty-six, transliterated from the Gullah by EK

SEVEN

It's still hours before dawn when I set out. Chef tries to come too, but Auntie Ondine and them make it plain this got to be done alone. Story they write in my book, say I got to go into the woods and find the dead Angel Oak tree—whatever that be.

Not much woods in Macon. Most got cut down to plant cotton. But Nana Jean say she'll help. Tell me to walk out past Molly's barns. When I do, the ground under me feel like it's changing. And before I know it, I'm thick in woods I know wasn't here before. Only these the strangest trees I ever seen: with branches growing blue bottles instead of leaves. I stare up at them and make out the trapped haints. When we was small, my brother showed me how to catch lightning bugs in jars. That's what they remind me of, twinkling so.

I pick my way through the strange woods, touching the rough bark and wondering if it's real. In my head, I recite the story Auntie Ondine wrote in my book: *To find the dead Angel Oak tree, you have to want to badly enough.* So I'm thinking up all the reasons I'm hunting it. This Grand

Cyclops we have to stop. Butcher Clyde and the Ku Kluxes. Rescuing Michael George. The offer Auntie Jadine sees me taking, betraying everything. Mostly, I think of Sadie. Remembering the light dying in her eyes like a blowed-out candle. It fires an anger in me like an animal clawing to get free.

It's as I blink away fresh tears that the dead Angel Oak tree appears. And I do mean appear, because one moment it's not there and the next, it is.

Whoever named it, named it proper. The tree bone white, glowing against the black night. Long knotted branches grow out from a thick trunk, going every which way like the twisted legs of a spider—some up or to the side, others sweeping across the ground. There's no leaves on them gnarled-up things neither. Instead there's bones. Skulls, rib cages, horns, all kinds, from different animals, hanging and swaying in the night breeze.

I have to drag my feet to keep going, walking between branches I feel might snatch me up. When I reach the trunk, I pull out Chef's trench knife, the only weapon I brung. I plunge it straight into the white wood, and thick sap the color and smell of blood oozes out. Tightening up my jaw and my belly, I stab again, and again, into wood that spatters me in soft flesh. When I get a good hole formed, I reach in hands to pry it apart. It look like raw muscle in there, moving about and alive. Trying not to gag, I push an arm in up to my shoulder, forcing the hole to grow until the side of my body can get in, then part of my leg. I gasp when the tree takes hold of me and gives a strong tug, sucking me halfway into its flesh. I fight, panicking. But that tree pulls again. Once, twice, swallowing me up.

I'm falling. Tumbling through darkness before landing on something hard—cheek-first. I cough, spitting out bits of what I don't want to imagine, a metallic taste coating my tongue and the scent of a butchery in my nose. My clothes and hair are soaked to my skin like I been swimming in a river of gore. I almost slip under the slickness of my Oxfords before rising to my feet and looking about.

Sure ain't Bruh Rabbit's laughing place, my brother whispers.

I'm standing in an empty corridor so white it looks bleached. It stretches far as I can see. I make out other corridors branching from it, and wonder if they endless too. There's an unnatural quiet, so all I can hear is my own breathing. Turning, I see I'm against a wall. It got a bloody gash on it like a wound—the hole I cut into this world.

"Traveling here the first time can be jarring," a voice slices into the silence.

I whirl back around to find someone standing in front of me. A colored man. He's tall, wearing an all-white suit, even white shoes. He got on a matching bowler pulled low and, strangest of all, a white blindfold over his eyes. But he stares like he sees me plain.

"You've caused a bit of a mess," he notes, waving white-gloved fingers at my feet. His voice got a fancy way of speaking, and never rises above a whisper.

I glance down, noticing my bloody footprints before looking back to him. Do he expect me to wipe it up?

"Messes attract the hound," he explains.

His head tilts upward, and I follow. There's something on the ceiling, so white and colorless it's almost invisible against the wall. Its body is joined together under a covering of bony armor. More limbs than I can count extend from its sides, and antennae longer than my arm twitch on a rounded head. A centipede is what comes to mind. Only wide as a motorcar, and long as—well, I can't say, because the rest of it disappears down a corridor. But *damn* long will do.

Everything in me howls to run—to get far away from this thing! But before I can let out one good cuss the man is right up on me. Don't recall seeing him move, but now he got something cold and sharp pressed under my chin.

"Shhh." He places a long finger to his lips. "The hound is a scavenger, meant to keep this hall sterile. It will scour you away, as any other impurity."

Even as he speaks, the centipede thing starts crawling down, detaching partly from the wall. I tense up as its antennae twitch about me, followed by mandibles working like a machine on an eyeless face. Its limbs stretch out, each ending in humanlike hands with slender fingers. They slide along my legs, back, arms, feeling about. I almost bolt, but the sharp thing at my chin presses harder, forcing me onto the balls of my feet.

It's a mercy when the creature moves on, the armored ridges of its back gliding along my thigh. The sharp thing is pulled away and my eyes follow a silver knife flicking close, like one of Molly's dissecting blades.

"The hound has mingled your scent with mine," the man says. "It will leave you unmolested, for now."

I turn to see the centipede thing working at the gash on the wall. Where its mandibles touch, blood vanishes and the wound starts knitting together. I look back to the man.

"Are you them? One of the Night Doctors?"

"When you set eyes on the lords of this realm, you will not need ask."

He turns, prepared to dismiss me.

"Then you Dr. Antoine Bisset?"

At hearing his name, he goes still. I go on, relating the story written in my book.

"Antoine Bisset. A colored physician, looking for the Night Doctors in old slave stories. You figured out they was real. Went searching for the dead Angel Oak tree. That was in 1937, in North Carolina. I come here from Macon, Georgia, in 1922. The ones who sent me, who tell me about you, say time don't matter here. Your tomorrow might not even be mine. But they claim you came looking for something, to understand a secret."

He turns back to me, first his head, then his body—like it just remember. "And what does your story say I came seeking?"

"Hate," I say. "You come looking to understand hate."

He stares at me from behind that blindfold. "Do you know the abandoned practice of humorism, passed down by the Hamites of Egypt to the Greeks and Romans? It held that each of man's bodily fluids governed a principle: blood for life; yellow bile the seat of aggression; black the cause of melancholy; and phlegm, apathy. I believe one humor is yet unaccounted for. What men call *hate*. You and I have seen too much to discount its existence."

"Did you find it? This source of hate?"

His jaw tenses. "I have hunted it in the entrails of men. Brought back specimens for my lords to feast upon, for I have introduced them to this delicacy. Yet still, its source eludes me."

"What if I could bring you hate? Not from people, but from . . . beings . . . like your lords. Things that carry hate pure in their blood. That live and thrive on it."

He's in front of me in a blur. No knife this time, but his blindfolded gaze feels as sharp—slicing at me, peeling back layers to inspect what's beneath. "Why would you come here to gift me such a thing?"

"Because I need your help." I tell him about the Ku Kluxes. About Butcher Clyde. "I need you to convince your lords, to help us fight," I finish.

"You are mistaken if you believe I hold sway over them."

"But you can offer a feast of this delicacy. Bet they like that."

He takes a while, then asks, "What will you give in exchange?"

My eyebrows raise. "Ain't the chance to feast enough?"

He grins, showing white teeth. "Do you know why the

lords of this place stole away slaves? Because misery fascinated them. The tear of it, the pain. And who had seen more misery than they? But I came here willingly, like you. So I was able to demand the chance to pay the price for what I sought." He grabs my hand quick, pressing it to his chest. There's no warmth there. No breathing. No heartbeat. Only . . . emptiness. As if he been carved out like a gourd. "The price I paid. You will need to pay your own."

I pull my hand free, remembering Auntie Ondine's warning, but nod. "Yes, I—"

All at once, something seizes me. I go down, my head smacking the floor. I see stars, then realize I'm moving. Someone got ahold of me, dragging me by my feet. I twist my head up in panic, thinking to find the centipede thing. But it's a different monster.

They look like men. No, giants. There's two of them, in long white robes. One has me by a six-fingered hand, pale skin stretched tight over bone. Remembering Chef's knife at my waist, I fumble for it, get it in my fingers, and plunge it into that hand. Don't even make a dent. But the one holding me turns a head about on a slender neck, and the fight drains out of me. No doubt about it—this is a Night Doctor.

The face looking at me is colorless and empty—no eyes or nose, no mouth even. Just wrinkled skin on a long head. A set of voices start in my ears, whispering like sliding knife blades. I go stiff, my body caught in ropes I can't see as I'm hoisted atop a flat block of stone. All about me are Night Doctors, staring down with their no-faces. My eyes all I can move, and I roll them about, like a frightened animal in a trap.

Dr. Bisset walks into my vision, small next to these giants. "As you came here of your own will, my lords will hear your petition of bargain." He leans in close. "But I cannot guarantee your leaving."

I try to open my mouth to speak, but find it still shut.

"No need. My lords have their own ways of understanding."

That whispering comes again. A whole lot of it. Can't move my eyes no more or even blink. I stare straight up to where another block of stone is descending. It got silver things stuck to it—one like a scissor, another a curved knife, others with needles and hooked ends. They look like things from Molly's laboratory. Like her dissecting table.

When the first cut comes to my belly, I'd scream if I could. The pain like nothing I ever felt, and the only thing in the world is that suffering. Those six-fingered hands pull me wide open, like they cleaning fowl. One reaches inside, lifting out something I think is my liver. They pass it bloody between them, running fingers along it, each bending to inspect in turn. Between my agony I can hear Dr. Bisset talking.

"My lords were the first practitioners of hepatoscopy, who taught it to the Babylonians and the priestesses of Saturn, to read the mysteries of the entrails. For it is here we keep our secrets hidden."

In my head, memories flash—watching a mob hunt

down colored folk in Elaine, Arkansas; Ku Kluxes rampaging down Greenwood in Tulsa; Sadie's face gone still. My misery, my pain, served up to these monsters on a plate. They read it all, like some witch sorting through a gutted possum. They cut and take, pulling out my bladder and ropes of glistening intestines, until I'm screaming even with my mouth closed, singing to them all the misery I seen. Somehow I can hear it, echoing through their white halls until blackness takes me.

When I open my eyes I'm at my house, looking at the door hanging off its hinges. My belly is whole, and I'm not covered in tree blood. But it's night. Always night.

"Interesting," a voice comes.

I jump, turning to find Dr. Bisset, standing where he don't belong.

"What you doing here?"

"Observing."

"Is this in my head? Or is it real?"

He glances to me behind his blindfold. "Would it make a difference?"

I see he been around haints enough to take up their sideways talking.

"Did *they* send me here?"

"There's something here my lords cannot see. Something you hold deep. It intrigues them. And that is rare." He turns, walking inside the house, forcing me to follow. He goes straight for the hatch and I overtake him, grabbing his arm.

"No! Not this."

But he pulls away, slippery as a fish, and throws open the secret door. His head cocks curious at the girl, before he offers a hand. I'm surprised when she takes it, climbing out the hole in a way she never would for me. She holding something—the silver hilt of my sword, with a jagged piece of black sticking out. So it's broken here too.

Dr. Bisset bends to one knee. "You've been in here a long time."

The girl nods. "It's where she keeps me."

"I don't keep you nowhere!" I snap, anger bubbling up.

She looks at me, and the fear in her round eyes sets me back.

"Why do you stay down there?" Dr. Bisset asks.

"To hide from the monsters. The ones who came looking."

"That was seven years ago!" I shout.

Dr. Bisset glances between us, and whatever he got under that blindfold put two and two together quick. "You look young for just seven years past," he tells the girl.

"She keeps me this way. Think it's easier to imagine me small."

"Then let us sweep away all illusions." Dr. Bisset waves a gloved hand, and the girl changes. She still in a night-shirt, but she's eighteen now. And she looks more like me. Not quite the woman of twenty-five, but no denying who she'll become.

"Now," he says, looking between us. "Tell me about the monsters."

When I don't speak, she do.

"They come one night, while we sleeping. Men, wearing white sheets and hoods. Daddy open the door holding his shotgun, and they start quarreling. My brother, he say they look like ghosts. But I can see them proper. They ain't men. They monsters. I try to tell mama, but my brother put me into the hatch."

I close my eyes, remembering the rest. The sounds of bullets going through Daddy and the door. The Ku Kluxes rampaging above me. Mama's screams. My brother's cries. Me in the hole, shaking with fright. That's when the sword first come. I still remember its coolness in my grip, sending visions in my head. It was humming with eagerness, willing me to get up there, to fight the Ku Kluxes. But I was so scared . . .

"—was like I couldn't move," the girl says, completing my thoughts. "Like something had ahold of me. I just stayed there in the dark, waiting for it to be over. Stayed down there almost two whole days. When I finally come out everybody was gone. So I went seeking—"

"No!" My heart beating fierce. "Don't give them this!"

Dr. Bisset don't even turn to me. "Where did you go seeking?"

My younger self stares me straight in my eyes when she betrays us. "The barn."

"Take me there." When I don't move, he sighs. "That wasn't a request." He grabs my arm and the world shifts, like I'm moving without walking. When I stop, we're out back. In front of the barn, where the door is open slight. It's morning now. Because that's when I came here.

"Why you want to see this?" I whisper.

"As I have told you, my lords desire the secret you keep from them, for which you have constructed quite the ruse."

"When they asked to see your misery, did you just show it to them?" I spit back.

He turns to me, moving a hand to lift his blindfold. I suck in a breath. Where his eyes should be, there's empty holes, raw and bloody. Like they was . . . plucked out.

"My lords wished to see the misery I had witnessed through my own flesh. They asked, and I willingly surrendered. Consider this intrusion . . . slight."

He walks to the barn door, pushing it open and stepping inside. I stay there breathing fast, feeling like I might drown. Slender fingers twist into mine and I look at my younger self. The fear on her face is gone, because I know it's all inside me now.

"We can do it together," she says. Then hands me the broken sword. "More yours than mine. Remember what I told you. They like the places where we hurt. They use it against us." With a gentle pull, she leads me to the barn door, forcing my feet forward.

When I step inside, I'm alone. Whatever she was—a ghost I left behind, some trick in my head—is gone. So it's through my eyes that I relive the cold December morning seven years back, when I entered to the terrible sight before me. Three bodies. My family. All hanging from the barn rafters by ropes. They swing in the morning sunlight, feet seeming to dance on the open air. Something grabs hard at my insides, and I fall to hands and knees, doubled over, reliving the horror and guilt.

"Such pain." Dr. Bisset is knelt down beside me. "Sadness for what you lost. Shame at what you could not do. And anger—so much anger." His empty eyes read me, boring into my deepest crevices. "You used that anger, fled from family and friends, then went seeking your vengeance, to etch your own story in blood."

I bite down, remembering. I stayed with my mama's people after. Whole time, the sword was with me, singing its secrets, teaching its deadly rhythms. When I was ready, I took off looking for Ku Kluxes. First one I killed, I poured much of the rage I held into its death. Hacked it to pieces. But wasn't enough. I had more pain and anger to give. Two years I spent wandering, killing Ku Kluxes. Don't know if I was even fully human no more. Was just the vengeance and killing. Now I hunted the monsters. I was somewhere in the Tennessee woods, descending into a hell of blood and slaughter, when Nana Jean's call dug me out that pit. Became a person again. But I buried the wound that fueled me deep, stuffing a little girl back into that hatch, and all the horrors she'd seen.

"I'm sorry," I whisper, to her, to myself.

"My lords find your misery . . . delectable," Dr. Bisset says. "You *are* a rare treat."

My eyes roll up to meet his empty sockets and a new

anger rises inside me. This is my pain. My scar to carry. Ain't theirs to feast on, to suck dry like marrow from a bone. I've had enough of monsters, devouring bits of me, trying to eat me up altogether.

"I hunt monsters," I tell him between clenched teeth.

I don't know when I extend my hand to call up my sword. I feel the broken piece I hold stir, fresh visions swirling in my head. More than I ever seen at once, coming and going in a blur. Once more there's the song. The beautiful, vengeful song. It's stronger too—hundreds of voices in harmony. They pull on those slave-selling chiefs and kings, to cry out and wake up slumbering gods. I look down to the jagged blade to find it covered in black smoke, growing to take the familiar leaf shape, binding together until the dark metal is mended and made whole. It's then I realize that amid the many visions, the girl is truly gone. No more frightful eyes. No more fear to pull me under. The wound I made of her is still there, but it don't pulse raw like it used to. It's mending too, even if it might never fully heal.

Dr. Bisset looks at the sword. And those emptied eyes somehow carry surprise.

"How—?" he begins, but I cut him off.

"This is my place. My pain. You got no right here! Your lords like misery so much? Let me show them!" The black leaf-blade explodes into brilliance as the song goes deafening. The light burns through everything, till I'm blinded.

When I can see again I'm back. In the dissecting hall. There's a new sound in my head—shrieking, from a dozen voices.

Too much! Too great! It is too much!

The Night Doctors. They bent over, hands to their heads, like they trying to block something out. Their power over me seems broken, and I can move and sit up. My shirt is open so I can see my belly. Everything is how it's supposed to be. Only sign my insides was ever spilled out is the tiniest scar I feel under one finger. In my other hand is something even more amazing. My sword!

It's as bright as it was in the dream place, and whole. The blade hums, vibrating as the souls drawn to it sing out their lives. These Night Doctors, who would snatch away slaves in their ones or twos, got more misery and pain coming from those songs than they ever know. And it's too much. I take some pleasure in seeing them squirm.

Then Dr. Bisset is there.

"Enough!" he snarls.

Suddenly I'm lifted up from the dissecting table and moving in that odd way he do down corridors. When we stop my back slams against a wall, the one I came through.

"You have overstayed your visit," he says. "Time to return."

"What about your lords? Will they help?"

"You are fortunate you still live after what you've done."

"We had a bargain! That you would talk to them for me!"

He leans forward, looking at me through the white blindfold he got back on. "Were I you, I would take what I have gained and never come back here again."

He gives a hard shove, and I fall into stone, passing through darkness, soft and fleshy, before tumbling onto earthen ground. I lift up to see I'm a ways behind Nana Jean's farmhouse. The forest of giant bottle trees is gone. And looming up before me, the dead Angel Oak tree is fading. I watch it go, before lying down to stare up into the night, clutching my mended sword to my chest.

EIGHT

It's raining the Sunday night we make our way up Stone Mountain.

Not no Presbyterian rain neither. I'm talking a shaking and hollerin' Baptist downpour.

We an odd bunch. Me and Chef. Emma and three of her "comrades," including two dark fellas she say Sicilians. Molly's apprentices, Sethe and Sarah, in wide-brimmed hats and rifles over their shoulders. Nana Jean here too, with Uncle Will and the Shouters. I tell that Gullah woman this no place for old folk, but she say they fixing to do some big root magic. And when she set her mind, no changing it.

Ain't easy going neither. Stone Mountain just as it's named: a dome of gray touching the sky. The bottom is surrounded by trees and shrubs. But the top is mostly bare stone and the trail we taking been turned into a mess of water and sediment. Flashlights help, but even then it's hard going. Traded my Oxfords for boots and gaiters, some moss-green knickers, a dark shirt, and a navy-blue poncho Molly stitched from rubbery cloth that hard to stay wet. Nana Jean sensed rain was coming, and had us pack proper. Seems her premonition more literal than I thought. Still envy Chef's soldiering outfit. Not to mention that hat what water just slide off of. I got my own brown cap pulled tight. Make it hard to see, but keeps the rain out my face.

About a half hour past we met with other bands who answered our call. Most from nearby Atlanta, veterans easy to pick out in their rain slickers and rifles with silver bayonets. Smaller groups come from Marietta and Athens. Even so, only about thirty of us can fight. Which ain't much.

I wonder about Dr. Bisset keeping our bargain. Though remembering his face when last I seen him, wouldn't bet on it. Memories of my insides being pulled out sends a hand to my stomach. Was that just a night ago? Took shifts with Chef in the six-hour drive from Macon. But what sleep I got was fitful, full of things I'd like forgetting. Now a dull ache weighs on my limbs. Not sure what keeping me going. Maybe just anger.

Sometimes I forget, and glance over to check on Sadie. I imagine the complaints she'd be making over this rain. Or the nonsense she'd be going on about—some story from her tabloids. Feels like them Ku Kluxes cut her right out this world, leaving behind a hole where she supposed to be. Now they got Michael George. It all set a fire burning hot enough in me I think the rain might sizzle on my skin.

Trees start getting sparse, leaving only steep wet rock ahead. That finally convinces Nana Jean to stop. Say she,

Uncle Will, and the Shouters to rest here and join us later. Chances of that is next to none. But fine by me. She puts a blessing on us before we go, leaving them sheltered under a crop of trees to make our way to the mountaintop.

Slippery don't begin to describe this climb. The bare rock feels smooth beneath me, and I fight to keep my footing. As we get closer, I can hear noise like someone talking as light reflects off the sky. It gets louder, blaring by the time we reach near the top. A man's voice booms into the night, competing with the rain. The anger in me boils as I recognize it. We gather everybody under a last patch of brush and trees, allowing them to catch their breath, while me and Chef creep forward to see what we arrived to.

The sight that greets us is out of a nightmare. A broad stretch of gray stone full of Klans. Never seen so many. Must be hundreds. They stand in rows, seeming unconcerned their robes getting soaked to the skin. Their hoods are pulled back, and wide, staring eyes are fixed straight ahead, at a movie playing on Stone Mountain.

The Birth of a Nation.

I asked Molly how they'd show a movie outside. She said all they needed was a projector that generated its own power and something to bounce the picture off of. Seems they built a screen. Thing must be fifty feet tall and twice as wide. Don't know where the projector is, but it's beaming moving pictures big as ever. At the bottom of the screen, a wooden platform been built. On it stand six men and women, with arms tied in front and sacks over their heads. My heart catches at seeing their dark limbs in the light coming off the screen. One got to be Michael George.

A giant cross of timber is propped up on the stone ground. And standing beside it on the platform is a man. Can't make out his face this far out. But he broad and big, recognizable enough in his Klan robes. Plus it's his voice we been hearing.

"Butcher Clyde." I spit.

Chef nods. "That him. Talking all kinds of nonsense."

That he is. This movie should have music blaring like an orchestra. Instead, there's Butcher Clyde, his voice echoing through the rain, going on about the white race and the like. The crowd stands there dazed, hanging on his every word, eyes glued to that great big screen.

"Must be Klans from all over," Chef mutters.

"And Ku Kluxes."

They ain't hard to spot, faces shifting and bending even through this downpour. Some spread out between the people. Others stand in long lines, holding fiery torches, the strange flames undisturbed by rain.

"So many in one place," Chef says. "Feels like Tulsa."

Look like Tulsa. All here to see their god be born.

Grand Cyclops is coming. When she do, your world is over.

"Something off with these Klans to you?" Chef asks. "The ones ain't turned?"

"You mean other than standing on top a mountain in a storm?"

"It's their faces. Don't look right."

Hard to see between the rain. But I lift my cap and squint, glimpsing faces in the light of the movie screen. There *is* something off with these Klans—different from the Ku Kluxes. Can't say what it is, though, or what it means.

"We don't have the numbers to take on all that," Chef says.

I look to her. No fear on her face. She seen too much for that. But there's an expectation that we won't win. She'll still go charging into the fight. Same with Emma, Molly's apprentices, and all those resistance folk we leading. Every last one, knowing they won't see the sun rise. Only, I'm not about to let that happen, if I can help it.

"I'm going out there."

Chef's face screws up. "Come again?"

"Butcher Clyde. You heard him last night. He invited me here."

"It's a trap. A hundred Ku Kluxes gonna come raging at the sight of you!"

I shake my head. "He want something from me. Been wanting it."

"What the hell he want from you?"

"To make an offer."

Chef stares like I done lost my head. I ain't told her or Nana Jean about this. But now I take a breath and speak all of it. She listens quiet, and when I finish takes a moment before saying, "Devil wouldn't be the devil if he didn't know how to tempt. You know what this offer is?"

I been thinking on that. About how Butcher Clyde slipped in my head that first time. Through that memory I kept locked deep.

I nod slow to Chef. "Think I do."

"Then you probably already made your choice."

There's a sudden *whoosh*! We look out to see the giant cross go up in flames. Just like the torches, that blaze seems untouched by rain, transforming the timber into a beacon of hellfire against the black night. I turn to Chef, catching its glare in her eyes.

"I have to go now. Maybe I can stop this."

"Or get yourself killed."

"Might be so. But I have to try." I remember Auntie Ondine's words. "Time to balance the world on the tip of a sword."

Chef looks at me hard, then says. "All right, then. But I'm coming with you."

I start to protest but she cuts me off. "Sadie wouldn't let you go out there by yourself, and I won't neither. Make peace with it, because we going over that trench together!"

I think of throwing a punch, knocking her clean out and taking off. More likely, though, she'd just whoop my behind. And I'm in no mood to take a licking before I face my possible death. I give in, guilty at feeling relief I don't have to do this alone.

"You never asked what choice I made about this offer."

Chef shrugs. She puts a Chesterfield to her lips, moving to light it before remembering the rain. "Got to trust the soldier next to you will do the right thing. No use worrying about it."

When I walk out onto the mountaintop it's still pouring, thick droplets forming pools on the stone ground. Chef beside me, in her Hellfighter uniform, the unlit Chesterfield clamped in her teeth. Don't think I been happier to see that easy smile. The rows of Klans keep their eyes stuck to the screen, ignoring us as we stroll a wide path up their middle. A Ku Klux holding a torch the first to see us. It peels back human lips and starts up squawking. Butcher Clyde's sermon cuts off from the platform and as one big beast, that whole sea of white turns in a ripple toward us.

We keep on, like we ain't two colored women walking into a pack of demons, human and otherwise. But none try to stop us. Not the Ku Kluxes. Nor the Klans neither, who definitely looking not just off but *wrong*. A knot grows in my stomach at that sea of wrong white faces. Something here I ain't put together yet.

I pull my eyes from them, reaching the platform.

Butcher Clyde stands there, rain-slick skin shining in the glow of the fiery cross and grinning down from under that suit of flesh.

"Maryse! We almost thought you might not come!"

That's a lie. He always knew. This whole thing like a story he been writing.

"Please come up! You arrived just in time! But just you. Don't need the spare."

"She comes with me!" I nod to Chef.

His smile tightens, but he waves a hand. "However you want it."

Together, me and Chef march up the platform steps. If you're thinking, it must be a strange thing, being who we are, to stand there in front of hundreds of hateful faces, I assure you it is. Some of the Ku Kluxes got their mouths open, drinking up rainwater while the Klans all got that wrongness to their faces. I turn back to Butcher Clyde, the movie behind us playing bigger than life while the flames of that unholy cross lick at my soul. My eyes go then to the others on the platform—six in a row, and colored. Take one glance to find who I'm looking for.

"Michel George!" I call. But he don't answer, don't even turn.

"Oh, your beau can't hear you," Butcher Clyde says. "None of them can."

He walks over to pull the sack off Michael George's head and there's relief and pain at seeing that familiar beautiful face, unharmed. Except . . .

"What you done to his eyes?" I demand.

"Oh, that?" Butcher Clyde moves a hand in front of Michael George's blank face. He don't flinch. Just stares out with white eyes, no pupils or nothing, as rain rolls down his dark skin. "Don't fret, he's just doing a kind of sleeping. But don't you worry. You do right by us, and we'll let him back to you, no worse for wear. The others . . . well, she's going to be a might *peckish* when she shows up."

She. This Grand Cyclops.

I stare into Michael George's empty face, craving to reach out and touch him, hold him. But that's what Butcher Clyde wants. I can see it in his grin, delighting at my pain. Clenching my fists to hold back the rage, I turn to the crowd.

"So this it, then? You call me here to see your little revival?"

Butcher Clyde's smile stretches into a jack-o'-lantern's grin. And I remember he just some things playing at being a person. "We've invited you to witness the grand plan."

"What I tell you the last time about your grand plan?"

He chuckles. "I believe your precise words were, 'Fuck your grand plan.' But we haven't told you the role you're to play in it. Wouldn't you like to know? We've been planning your part so long."

When I don't answer he goes on.

"As you know, we specialize in that thing you call *hate*. To your kind, it's just a feeling. A bit of rage behind the eyes that can drive you to commit all sorts of beautiful violence. But for us, those feelings are a power of their own. We feed on it. Treasure it as life." He turns to the gathered Klans. "Look at all that delightful hate. We didn't put it there, was always growing inside. Just gave it a nudge to help it blossom. A few reels of celluloid and they come to us whole and willing. But sustaining as that hate is, it's not very . . . potent."

I raise an eyebrow. Seem these Klans can hate well enough.

"You see, the hate they give is senseless. They already got power. Yet they hate those over who they got control, who don't really pose a threat to them. Their fears aren't real—just insecurities and inadequacies. Deep down they know that. Makes their hate like . . . watered-down whiskey. Now your people!"

His eyes light up, and he steps closer.

"Y'all got a good reason to hate. All the wrongs been done to you and yours? A people who been whipped and beaten, hunted and hounded, suffered so grievously at their hands. You have every reason to despise them. To loathe them for centuries of depravations. That hate would be so pure, so sure and righteous—so strong!"

His body shudders, like he imagining the sweetest wine.

"What I got to do with any of that?"

"Oh, Maryse, you're our top candidate!"

The confusion on my face stretches his grin impossibly wider.

"Told you we've been watching you. We knew those interlopers were going to crown a champion to wield their little magic against us, as they done before. But what if we could guide that choice? Instead of fighting their champion, we could help mold her. Let her see what it's like to hurt. Let that wound fester. So that she keeps that little seed of hate deep inside. Then we feed it. Water it with our dogs. Let her hunt them, kill them, and enjoy it. And you do enjoy it, don't you? Why, that hate will keep growing until it's good and strong, waiting to be harvested, waiting for you to just *tap* into it."

The rage in me shakes my voice. "This the part where you make your offer?"

"Indeed it is," he purrs.

"Well, no need, I know what it is! And I don't want it! Not from you!" He looks at me funny. And the heat in me rises higher. "You offering to bring back my family! Power over life and death, you said. Give me what I want more than anything. You think offering me that can make me switch sides? Come over to you? After what you done!"

There's a quiet from Butcher Clyde, which is unusual. All I can hear is my own deep, angry breathing and the beating rain. Then he does something unexpected. He laughs. Real hard. So that he's almost doubled over, slapping his thighs. And I imagine all those hidden mouths laughing too. He looks up at me, wiping away tears or rainwater.

"Oh, Maryse! You have quite the imagination! Bring your family back? That's what you've been thinking our offer is? Hoping for it? We can't bring your family back." His mirth cuts off and he turns cold serious. "They dead and gone. Forever."

His words wound like I didn't know words could, tearing into the deepest part of me. I feel my cheeks heat in shame. He's right. I had been hoping for it, yearning it, even as I struggled and fought not to take it. I wanted a thing like that to at least be possible. To know there was the chance.

"No, Maryse, you misunderstood our meaning," Butcher Clyde goes on. "You see, we're not asking you to switch sides. We're offering to come over to you."

I blink, his words chasing everything out my head. "What?"

He stares intently with those gray eyes. "Be our champion, Maryse. Lead our armies. Give your people the one thing they lack—"

"Hate?" I cut in.

"Power," he corrects, voice now intense. "What I told you all along. You bring us their righteous justified hate, and we will grant you power—enough to never need fear anyone again. Power enough to protect yourselves and defeat your foes, to make them cower and tremble before you in true fear. Power to avenge all those wrongs. Power over life and death, yours and your enemies!"

I stare, speechless. There it is—the offer. One I never saw coming.

"What about them?" I gesture to the gathered Klans.

"They already served their purpose."

"And this Grand Cyclops? She fine with you switching sides?"

His grin returns. "Who's grand plan do you think this is?"

"I came here to stop her. From coming to this world!"

"Stop her?" He laughs again. "But, Maryse, she's already here!"

I follow as he sweeps an arm to the crowd of Klans, at first not understanding. Then I see it again, the wrongness in all those faces. As if answering a summons, one in the front steps forward, looking up with a blank gaze as rain streams lines down his face. Then he starts to shaking, his whole body convulsing—before he collapses.

I hear Chef curse beside me, but my eyes are on that Klan, or what used to be him. His white robes lay there on the wet ground, and from inside slithers out what looks like raw, bloody flesh without no shape or form. Like his body been turned inside out. It crawls across the wet stone just as another Klan steps forward and does the same, then another, and another, and—

"What you do to them?" I ask, holding my belly from heaving.

"Why, we only gave them the sustenance they craved. This they did to themselves all too willingly. Like I told you already, they're just meat to us."

Meat. What he was feeding them in his shop. The living flesh.

"She's already inside them," he boasts. "They swallowed her up, fed her on their hate. Now she comes to claim her due."

I watch as the oozing mounds of flesh slither their way to the burning cross. They reach up, wrapping about the flaming timber, sending up an awful stink that burns my nose. In moments they all over it, one atop the next, until the heat of that undying hellfire fuses them to the wood and each other. Looks like a giant hand is sculpting them, piling that flesh onto a skeleton like clay, pulling and shaping it into something with long fleshy limbs, a torso extending across the ground, and curving body, growing taller and bigger by the moment. The Klans that come to join now don't even collapse no more. They just walk into the wall of living flesh and get sucked in whole. I can see them in there, bodies dissolving, so all that's left is their faces, mouths wide as if they screaming—screaming forever. When it finally stops, I bend my neck to stare up at the monstrosity born this night, rain pelting my face like the heavens weeping.

The Grand Cyclops don't look like nothing I ever seen. It reminds me of a long, coiling snake. But it got arms too, thick trunks that split into curling and writhing tentacles. The whole of her is made of people, their flesh now bound to her service, her vessel into this world. All along that awful body mouths open to let out a shriek of birth and triumph that shakes me to my bones.

"Isn't she beautiful?" Butcher Clyde asks, face like he caught the ghost.

The mouths on the Grand Cyclops all open and shriek again. No, not just shrieking. Talking, in an ungodly chorus.

We come to claim what is ours. This world. Bring forth our champion. Let us see!

"She wants to meet you, Maryse!"

Just as he says it the Grand Cyclops lowers her neck, until the stump where a head should be is bent just above me. A hundred eyes open up in her rippling flesh, every last one all too human. They squirm through her body like tadpoles swimming through muck, until they reach the stump, pooling into one big mass and focusing on me.

Behold the one who will accept our gift—our blessings.

The Grand Cyclops spreads out her arms, those writhing tentacles enveloping me within. Little nubs like human fingers break out along their length, and I can feel them sticky and wet sliding across my clothes and skin—touching, feeling, sizing me up. If a giant centipede with man hands hadn't done near the same to me a night previous, pretty sure I might have passed out then and there.

Yes! Oh yes! This one carries the anger of her people. Pure yet untapped. We could do much with this. We could do much for you!

"You only have to say yes, Maryse," Butcher Clyde urges. "Accept this gift!"

Should be easy for me to say no. To damn these monsters to hell and beyond.

But . . . Butcher Clyde's words are in my head and I can't shake them out. What they offering me is power. Power to protect. Power to avenge. Power over the life and death of my people. When colored folk ever had anyone offer us so much? When we ever had the power not to be scared no more? Ain't we been suffering and dying all this time, at the hands of monsters in human form? What difference then if we make a pact with some other monsters? What we owe this world that so despises and brutalizes us? Why lift a hand to save it when it ain't never done a damn thing to save us?

So close you are to seeing the truth, the Grand Cyclops croons. *Give over your anger. Let us show you how to wield it. How to make you strong. Without fear of your enemies or mercy. Do not flee from it. Embrace it. Who is to blame for the hate that hate made?*

I can feel the heat of that anger rising, hot enough to burn. In my head are all the visions I ever seen. Men, women, and children who look like me, under the lash, in chains, whipped until the flesh hanging from their bones, hurt so bad their souls cry out. This why they chose me. Because I carry not just the anger of what I seen with my own eyes but centuries of anger—growing up in me. Auntie Ondine's fears was right. In giving me that sword, they were molding me for the very enemy I'm meant to fight.

Be careful now, Bruh Rabbit. My brother's voice comes so strong, it feels like he's right in my ear. *We the trickster—the spider, the rabbit, even the fox. We fool those stronger than us. That's how we survive. Watch out you don't get tricked yo'self!*

His voice is followed by another.

They like the places where we hurt. They use it against us.

The words of the girl, my other self from the dream

place, strikes with sudden understanding. The places where we hurt. Where *we* hurt. Not just me, all of us, colored folk everywhere, who carry our wounds with us, sometimes open for all to see, but always so much more buried and hidden deep. I remember the songs that come with all those visions. Songs full of hurt. Songs of sadness and tears. Songs pulsing with pain. A righteous anger and cry for justice.

But not hate.

They ain't the same thing. Never was. These monsters want to pervert that. Turn it to their own ends. Because that's what they do. Twist you all up so that you forget yourself. Make you into something like them. Only I can't forget, because all those memories always with me, showing me the way.

I smile, and a cleansing breath cools the fire beneath my skin. This was my test. And I think I just passed. I flick eyes to Butcher Clyde.

"You said tonight, they all just meat."

He look confused for once. I appreciate that.

"That's what you call these Klans, just meat."

"Not sure we follow—"

"First time, back at your shop, you said *we* was all meat. No matter the skin. You say we all here for you to use up." I nod to the Ku Kluxes. "You'd do to us what they let you do to them. If I gave you the chance. That right?"

He don't answer, just puts on a jack-o'-lantern grin. But

it speaks well enough. I smile back, lowering my hand—and call up my sword.

The visions swirl about. Only there's no frightened girl threatening to pull me under. And with that fear conquered, seems like I opened a floodgate. The spirits that come now not just a few, not even hundreds. More like thousands, rushing to the sword, pouring out the songs of their lives, the strength of it running through the iron and up into me. Drums and shouts and cries, shrieks and laughter and howls, rhythmic chants and long keening moans. An archive of endless memories, from watery graves in the Atlantic to muddy rice fields and cotton plantations, from the stifling depths of gold mines to the sickly sweet smell of boiling sugar that consumed up people, devoured them in jaws of whips and chains and iron implements to shackle and ruin. I'm swept up by that maelstrom and I'm singing too, spilling out my own pain. The bound chiefs and kings shout at our cries, rousing old gods, and the cool silver slides into my waiting grip, black smoke stitching into a sharp leaf-blade. Somewhere near I hear Butcher Clyde choke, his voice strangled.

"We broke you!"

Don't know if he means me or the sword. Maybe both.

I wink at Chef before turning back to the Grand Cyclops, whose tentacles still writhing about me.

What is this? What is happening?

"You ever hear the story of Truth and Lies?" I ask. "Well, I'll get to the good part. You the Lie."

Bringing up my sword, I grip it with both hands and plunge it into that nest of eyes on the monster's stump of a head. The blade bursts into light, scorching all it touches. The Grand Cyclops shudders as white fire courses through her massive body, showing beneath the glistening flesh, sending hundreds of mouths screaming in agony, flames erupting from their parted lips. Across the mountaintop, Ku Kluxes scream too, like they feeling that pain. Good! I pull out my sword just as she whips back her long neck, sending blood and charred flesh flying.

Chef whoops. "That's what I'm talking about!" She pulls out two bottles from her jacket, shaking them until the liquid inside glows bright. A special concoction Molly helped brew: part explosives and pure Mama's Water. Running forward she hurls one into a screaming flaming mouth on the Grand Cyclops's torso and then the second into another. When she drops to the platform, I follow, just as the detonations go off—blowing big holes in the monster's body, so that I think she might come crashing down. But she bellows a roar that shakes the mountaintop. And I know, we only done made her mad.

I stand up just as something jumps past me and I realize it's one of the Klans. I look down to see more swarming and climbing up the platform. But they not coming for me or Chef. They running to the Grand Cyclops, leaping to meet her and getting sucked into that flesh, their bodies healing the damage.

"Shit!" Chef says.

She don't get another word out as a tentacle whips out, hitting her full on to send her flying. I shout as she goes spinning into the night. Then a whole mass of tentacles rain down, tearing apart half the movie screen and smashing the platform, taking me and whoever else down in a shower of splintered wood.

The world goes spinning and it seems forever before it stops. I lift up from where I land, bruised all over, to crawl from beneath the debris. Lost my cap, and now I blink away rainwater looking for Chef. Michael George got to be here too. I make it to my knees, to find the Grand Cyclops waiting, raised to her full awful height. With the screen torn near to shreds, moving pictures reflect off her body— ghostly images of Klans riding horses across translucent flesh. She bends down, glaring with one mass of endless eyes burning with anger. No, that there's hate.

You would deny us! Wound us! We will wipe you from this world!

I raise up, planting feet firm and lifting my sword.

"Well." I pant slow. "Don't take all day."

But those mass of eyes not looking at me no more. Something else caught their attention. I turn to see a figure stepping sideways out of nothing, his body flat as paper before filling out into a brown-skinned man in an all-white suit and a matching bowler cocked to the side.

Dr. Bisset.

"You're late."

Notation 7:

When President Lincoln send out the emancipation, the stingy masters them didn't want the slaves to learn about it. But slaves had they own ways of knowing. One named John, he raised up in the kitchen, and stole away how to read watching missus teach her young'uns. He come with a letter on the emancipation, and everybody in the cabins gather 'round as he read. That's why we call this Shout *Read 'em, John, Read 'em* for the day he come to tell the people about they freedom!

—Interview with Uncle Will, age sixty-seven, transliterated from the Gullah by EK

NINE

Dr. Bisset stands there blindfolded, not a bit wet, like the rain afraid to touch him.

"There is no early or late with us," he answers. "Just a matter of time."

He definitely been around them haints too long. Wait—*us*?

The dead Angel Oak tree up and appears right behind him, branches going every which way across the mountaintop. Around it stand half a dozen figures, untouched as well by the rain and too tall to be men, with wrinkled skin for faces.

Night Doctors.

The Grand Cyclops roars, endless mouths gnashing teeth as she pushes past me to meet this threat. One of the Night Doctors lifts an arm to throw out a bone-white rope of chain with a curved hook. It latches onto her trunk, digging in and pulling. She brings down a thick tentacle, crushing the Night Doctor flat and throwing up chunks of stone. A second tentacle crushes another. My heart drops, thinking she killed them dead. But the two slide out from under the tentacles and stand back up, whole! Just like that! They lift arms to throw new chains, one hook catching the Grand Cyclops's neck and another latching to a snarling mouth. More chains fly, each digging into her monstrous body. Something shimmery travels down those links to the Night Doctors that quivers their wrinkled faces, and I realize they feeding on her. Feeding on her hate, and the hate of all the people that make her up. It must hurt something fierce, because all those mouths scream. Not in rage no more, but pain. And fear.

She tries to pull free, scrambling back. But the Night Doctors already turned away, chains slung over their shoulders. Some Ku Kluxes shed their human skins, running to protect their god. But the Night Doctors swat them away one-handed or snap their necks like chickens. Them frightful beings never stop their stride, walking into the dead Angel Oak tree one by one. The Grand Cyclops is dragged along, caught like a fish even as she struggles to break free, dozens of human hands erupting from her body to grab hold at anything. But there's only the smooth mountaintop, and those fleshy fingers skitter across stone and rainwater in vain.

When she reaches the tree its bleached-white trunk opens wide, like a gaping mouth. The Grand Cyclops's tentacles lash at the branches, trying to tear off limbs, desperate as she sends out frightened shrieks. But it's no use. That dead tree swallows her up, where the dissecting hall waits. Bet she not gon' like that. Under my breath, I whisper Chef's ditty:

Night Doctors, Night Doctors
You can cry and carry on.
But when they done dissectin'
Every bit of you is gone.

"A bargain kept," Dr. Bisset's voice comes. Then a pause. "On your left."

It's the only warning as a silver cleaver slices for my neck. I jump back, bringing up my sword in time to block it. Butcher Clyde. He wearing his true face now—eyes turned to orifices ringed with teeth, while more mouths howl under his wet robes, spitting their rage.

"You betrayed us! Ruined our plans!"

He so mad he not so much fighting as battering me with those cleavers. But they powerful strong, striking dazzling sparks off my sword.

"Going to kill you! Then eat you! Make you meat!"

A rumble bubbles up from somewhere deep inside him and the front of his robes shred away, revealing a gaping mouth where his belly should be—same one from my dream! It opens to show curving teeth like needles, and a long, darting tongue. That nasty thing shoots out at me, and I slice it clean off, leaving it flopping in the rain. Been waiting to do that. He screams, staggers, then comes at me again, mouths open and singing.

It's like the night at the juke joint. A mashed-up chorus, with no real timing or rhythm. As if it was created to unmake music. Like before it threatens to take me off balance, and I stumble under it. But no! I got songs too! I listen to my sword, letting those chanting voices fill me up. For a moment it seems the two are battling: my songs and his uneven chorus. But it was never a real fight. What I have is beautiful music inspired by struggle and fierce love. What he got ain't nothing but hateful noise. Not a hint of soul to it. Like unseasoned meat. My songs crash right through that nonsense, silencing it, just as my sword takes off his arm. He falls back and I dip low, slicing away everything under one knee.

When he lands on his back I walk over, watching him fight to get up. Dr. Bisset appears beside me, studying the thing on the ground with interest. I bend close, easily avoiding the cleaver slashing at me uselessly. His mouths hiss, and I get to work, hacking away at the meat of him, the lie of him, all to the beautiful songs in my head. About halfway through, his whole body falls apart. Pieces of flesh go slithering and crawling out across the mountaintop, like a broken hive of insects seeking escape.

But Dr. Bisset is there—a blur, everywhere at once. He picks up each one of those pieces, dropping them into what looks like a white medical bag. When he's done the bag the same size but bulging, as shrieking things inside fight to get out. He nods and I follow his meaning to a small dark shape in the distance, fleeing for the trees below. Butcher Clyde's head by that red hair, grown legs like tubes. I catch up with it quick, planting a foot atop his forehead. Under the heel of my boot, two mouths where eyes should be gnash jagged teeth.

"Didn't I say that one day I was going to cut you to pieces?"

When he open his other mouth wide to snarl I plunge my sword inside. The blade goes hot and there's a melding of shrieks as Butcher Clyde's head smokes and chars from the inside. I don't stop until there's quiet and nothing but a lump of ash that the rain begins to wash away.

"A shame," Dr. Bisset says. "I would have liked to examine that specimen."

I look to his bag. "You ain't got enough?"

He answers with a tip of his bowler, then walks toward the dead Angel Oak tree.

"How did you convince your lords?" I call out. "To help I mean?"

He glances back. "I've told you. You intrigue them. They will be keeping . . . a watch on you."

Now *that*, I don't like one bit.

He sets out again, his body turning sideways when he reaches the dead Angel Oak, going flat as paper once more. Then he and the tree, fade from the night. The full weight of all that just happened almost drags me to my knees. Then I remember.

Chef! Michael George!

It takes some digging to find them. First Chef. She got a nasty bump on her head. Out cold, but still breathing. I come across two other women before finding Michael George. He bruised some, but alive. Though his eyes still turned up into white marbles. I look to the sky, catching rain on my face. The Grand Cyclops is gone. Butcher Clyde too. But this don't feel over. Right about then I realize, we not alone.

I turn to find a mass of Ku Kluxes. The Klans who didn't give their bodies to the Grand Cyclops still fixed on what's left of the movie screen. But these monsters hiding behind men's faces all looking dead at me in the pouring rain. I remember what Butcher Clyde called them—dogs. Now with no master.

One in front growls, flinging away the torch he's holding and changing into a full Ku Klux. Behind him follows another. And another. In moments they all changed. A hundred Ku Kluxes, maybe more, snarling and working into a frenzy. When I lift my sword, they go crazy, and all come running, like they plan on burying us under their pale bodies.

But a sudden cry goes up and I look out through the rain to see a hell of a sight.

Charging across the mountaintop is Emma Krauss and her comrades. Molly's apprentices, Sethe and Sarah, follow at their sides. And behind them come the rest, led by veterans in soldiers' uniforms, holding rifles with bayonets, a burly colored man at their front. We'd told them to stay put and wait for our signal. Guess they took all that just happened for that. The veterans move in fast strides, splashing water as they holler, passing up Emma and her people. Only Sethe and Sarah match the pace of those men, and together they smash into the Ku Kluxes.

The veterans go about like men at work, bringing down

Ku Kluxes and stabbing with bayonets. Sethe and Sarah are right hand and left hand, shooting Ku Kluxes and slashing out with big silver-edged knives. One comes too close and takes a blade across the throat, followed by a bullet through the eyes. Emma out there working the shotgun almost as fierce as Sadie. She blows a hole straight through one Ku Klux, then spins to shoot the leg off another. It crashes, and the soldiers' silver bayonets on it in a flash. The flames from discarded torches catch light of shredded robes and bits of platform, starting small, unnatural bonfires that make the mountaintop look like a picture out a war. All that fighting finally breaks some Klans from their trance. They stumble about, looking stupefied and backing away from the widening battle.

Me, I got my hands full. Ku Kluxes coming from every side. My sword sings as I swing wide, taking off reaching claws and slashing through flanks. Anything to keep them off me, with Chef and Michael George still unconscious at my feet. These monsters too stupid to coordinate without direction. I drive one or two into each other, and they get to scrapping. All about me bullets fly. Men and women scream. And Ku Kluxes go down.

But they not the only ones.

People fall too. The burly veteran gets dragged down by Ku Kluxes even as he stabs with a bayonet. One of Emma's comrades wounded bad, screaming as she pulls him to her while reloading the shotgun. Sethe and Sarah back to back now, Ku Kluxes circling like hounds.

Not going too good over by me neither. I'm breathing hard, two days of weariness taking their toll as I try not to slip on rain-slick stone. Every swing turning my arms to jelly, and the monsters keep coming: a pale-white tide of senseless hate. A damn shame, after everything, to have it end like this. A cut on my brow sends blood trickling into my eyes and I blink, opening them again to find the world now quiet.

The Ku Kluxes about me gone still as statues. Not just them, the whole mountaintop. People and monsters in the night, unmoving yet grappling in the heat of battle, making for a mad painting splashed across a black canvas. I look up to find tiny jewels in the air I realize are raindrops, and wonder if I could reach out and pluck one.

"You ever think on what Ku Kluxes do when they ain't, well, Ku Kluxing?"

The voice sends me stiff. Because it shouldn't be possible. But when I turn, the impossible standing right there. Sadie, thumbs tucked into her overalls as she studies a pouncing Ku Klux.

"Do they still go to work? Do their husbandly duties with their wives and—"

"Sadie." I practically breathe her name. "Sweet mercy! How . . . Am I dead?"

She rolls them big brown eyes. "Don't be a goose, Maryse, I'm the one dead."

And now I notice her yella skin, carrying a soft warm glow. Still, I doubt my eyes.

"Is this real?"

"Me standing here the *strangest* thing you seen tonight?"

She got a point. A deep sadness fills me up at seeing her face again.

"Oh, Sadie, it's my fault."

"How you figure?"

I swallow down my guilt. "I hadn't gone and provoked Butcher Clyde, maybe you wouldn't—"

"Maryse Boudreaux! Don't you go ruining my grand death with your moping! I made my own choices! You leave me that!"

I nod slow. "Just wish you wasn't. Dead, I mean."

She sighs. "Yeah, wish I wasn't too. Anyway, heard that Gullah woman calling. Just like when she gather us up. Seem that voice can reach farther than we ever know. Had to be here, though. Molly right, 'bout this place being a doorway. Only, we couldn't cross over—not till you made the right choice. Told the others you wouldn't take no offer from that old evil haint!"

I try to make sense of all she's saying. "Others?"

I follow her gaze to find men and women gathering, all carrying that same warm glow. They step right out the night amid the stillness of the mountaintop, between droplets of rain. I know right off who these people are, because my sword starts humming. These the spirits of folk murdered by Ku Kluxes and the hate they stir up. People who been—

I clutch my chest as one walks toward me. He my height, got dark eyes like mine, and those same rounded lips. His white shirt tucked into plain brown trousers held by suspenders, as he moves with a carefree stroll, face split in a crooked grin.

My voice comes choked. "Martin?"

"How you doing, Bruh Rabbit?" my brother answers, and my legs give way.

I sit staring, before reaching with trembling fingers that slip right through him.

"Tee-hee! Watch it now, that tickles!" His familiar chuckle sends me sobbing and laughing at once, and I turn, searching the ghost people. "Mama? Daddy?"

He shakes his head. "Not everybody crosses over. But they send their love."

So many words on my lips but what comes out is, "I'm sorry I couldn't save you."

He squats down close, eyes shimmering. "What happen to us, only the ones who done it to blame. We proud of you. So proud! You got nothing to be sorry for, you hear?"

I nod slow, then reach fumbling into a back pocket, pulling out a wet, beat-up thing and feeling silly as I offer it forward. "Still got your book. Put new stories in it too."

He laughs again and I treasure the sound of it. "Bet you do!"

"I miss you so much," I whisper.

His face softens. "I'm never far. Ain't you heard me talking, Bruh Rabbit?"

My eyes go wide and he winks.

"You so wrapped up in your grief, no other way you

would listen, except through them stories. Time to lay your burdens down. Live your life."

I nod tearfully, and he stands to look out across the mountaintop at several figures approaching. At first I think they more spirits. Because one in front glowing bright. But then I catch sight of that haint-blue dress, and bushy, crinkly white hair.

"Nana Jean?" That old Gullah woman strolling easy through unmoving Ku Kluxes and people, like she walking to church on Sunday. Uncle Will and the Shouters follow behind. How they even make it up that slippery mountain?

"Never doubt stubborn old folk," Sadie says to my unspoken question.

My brother smiles. "You done good, Bruh Rabbit. Now let us handle this."

He leaves a ghostly kiss on my cheek, before leaving to join the gathering spirits. They clustered around Nana Jean and the Shouters, reaching out to touch the old woman with ghostly fingers.

Sadie sits down beside me, grinning. "You gon' like this!"

Time comes rushing back. The rain, the cries, the battle. The Ku Kluxes all set to close in when a deep moan goes up. Nana Jean. Her voice seem to call to them and they whip about. She moans again and the ghost people around her take it up: a deep vibrating hum that pushes out through the air, parting the rain before it. Then that Gullah woman lifts her head to the heavens and cries out the song of a Shout.

Nana Jean's voice like thunder, a sound to shake your soul, moving to the beating heart of the world. The ghost people answer, and the Shouters start clapping, as the Stick Man pounds the mountain like a drum. The ghost people start to circling round the Gullah woman: a backward clock of feet sliding and shuffling, but never crossing. Nana Jean sings a song about the end times and it's like I can see her words taking shape. Signs etched on leaves as rocks cry out. A fiery horse without a rider burning tracks in a valley. Angels taller than hills perched on a spinning chariot wheel. The Gullah woman keeps crying out, and the ghost people give answer, the Shout moving faster in that ring.

The hairs on the back of my neck raise up as Nana Jean's Shout sends out more magic than I ever seen. My sword shakes in my hand as the spirits drawn to the blade rush to the circle, joining the Shout. Even those slaving chiefs and kings come, seeking their redemption. Together with the ghost people they whirl faster and faster about Nana Jean, becoming a blinding blur in the night. The Ku Kluxes screech in rage, hurling themselves at the spinning light, trying to reach Nana Jean and the Shouters, but it burns them up straight to ash. That light ain't nothing they can stop. It ain't nothing they can endure. This the Truth I know. And no Lie can stand against it.

Some Ku Kluxes got sense enough to realize the danger, and turn to flee. But that light is a cyclone now, spinning out to catch them. From inside that brilliance, I hear the

Gullah woman singing, taunting the Ku Kluxes who running, telling them there's no hiding place. The ghost people give answer, their voices a power to tremble the earth, as Ku Kluxes burn, the light cleansing their evil from the mountain. The Shout keeps going, whirling into the night. Like Judgment Day.

When there's not a Ku Klux left standing, the Shout vanishes. The ghost people gone with it, my brother too, their magic lingering in the air like lightning. All that's left is Nana Jean, spent from wielding so much magic, Uncle Will and the Shouters supporting her.

Sadie whoops. "Told you you'd like it!"

I shake my head in wonder. I ain't ever doubting that old Gullah woman again.

"Well, time for me to go too," Sadie says, standing.

My mouth opens, not knowing what to say. So I settle for the truth. "I miss you."

Sadie grins. "You betta. Y'all remember to do something big for me like I asked." She looks down. "What wrong with Cordy?"

I turn to where Chef still unmoving. "She got hit."

Sadie leans in. "There's a trick to this." And slaps Chef's face. But her fingers go right through. Frowning, she tries again, this time making a loud *smack,* and Chef bolts up with a start. Sadie laughs like it's the funniest joke in the world.

"My grandpappy was right." She winks. "We do get them back." Two wings unfurl from her behind her: beautiful gold feathers with streaks of black. She spreads them wide, lifting and shooting into the air like an arrow, gone.

"Guessing I missed a few things?" Chef asks, both of us staring up at the sky.

Someone groans. I look to find Michael George, coming awake. He opens eyes that are bright and brown and beautiful, blinking at me in confusion.

"Maryse?"

I kiss him so strong it leaves him startled. Only answer I got for now.

"It stopped raining," Chef notes.

I pull away from Michael George, looking around. She right. No more storm. Clouds clearing up so you can even see stars. On the mountaintop, no fires or Ku Kluxes left, but still Klans. Lots milling about, like ducks what got hit on the head. More on hands and knees, retching their guts out. Hope they spit up some of their own hate too.

Chef calls to our people, who locate the kidnapped colored folk amid the wrecked platform. At some point, Emma finds that projector and blows it to bits with her shotgun. The night goes pitch-black but at least we don't have to see that damned movie no more. When we got everybody, we set out. This time Nana Jean and the Shouters lead, and we follow Uncle Will's voice calling, "Adam in the Garden!" as the Basers answer, "Picking up leaves!"

Chef can walk some, but Michael George still weak. So I got to support them both. We ain't gone a ways before I notice a woman. Only Klans not stumbling around or retching. She kneeling in her robes, hugging a little boy close. Her eyes meet mine, bright and feverish. I recognize their faces. From Butcher Clyde's. Must not have eaten no meat. Seems my interruption that day saved them a bellyache, and worse.

"Monsters!" she stammers to me. "They was monsters! I seen them! I seen them!"

Chef and I look at each other, then answer back, "'Bout damn time!"

We leave her there to her newfound sight, making our way home.

EPILOGUE

I sit sipping the best mint julep I ever tasted. Just enough bourbon and sugar. Not a *real* mint julep, of course. Nothing here real. Not the antique white table or the wicker chair I'm sitting in, set on a mound of grass in what look like a swamp. The giant red oak still there, now covered in tresses of tan Spanish moss and lavender wisteria. Behind us sits a mansion, with ivy twisting about faded white columns and creeping across stone.

Auntie Ondine across from me, in an old-timey white dress and broad white hat. She's sipping her own mint julep while holding open a white ruffled parasol. Said they needed a change of scenery. I look up through the moss and wisteria, catching sight of Auntie Jadine perched on a branch. Her bare legs swing under the lace trim of her dress, brown toes wriggling while she hums, twirling her parasol.

Back at the table, Auntie Margaret jabbing her umbrella at me. Had the fool idea of asking why come foxes always up to no good in stories. Lord, if that didn't set her off.

"And them tales got it backward! Rubbish and rabbit propaganda is all that is!" She slams down her parasol, rattling a vase of snow-white carnations.

"Well!" Auntie Ondine's plump cheeks dimple kindly. "Before we started down that path, I believe I was asking how things are at home. Your battle with the enemy must have caused quite the stir!"

Yeah, about that. Things have been . . . strange.

Been four days now, and Georgia papers still carrying stories about "big happenings" on Stone Mountain. That there was a fire at a Klan rally, killing dozens. Others say it was a bad batch of moonshine poisoning. More claim it was a fresh outbreak of Spanish flu, explaining why the government showed up, burning bodies.

Turns out that last one's not so wrong. Leastways about the government.

Word come from Atlanta that the United States Army all over Stone Mountain. Got the place cordoned off with military trucks and soldiers. Scientists too, wearing gas masks and sweeping about with funny gadgets. All of them supervised by government men in dark suits, smoking and giving orders. Not just Stone Mountain either. They come to Macon.

Not army trucks but wagons. Full of men claiming to be Prohibition agents. They raided Butcher Clyde's shop, busting up liquor barrels and making a big to-do, charging he was a bootlegger. But me and Chef checked it out from a rooftop. Them government men was there, directing agents to seal up all that butcher meat in glass containers, packing them into wagons and driving off.

"So Sadie's claims proved correct," Auntie Ondine says when I finish.

I know. Hardly believe it myself. Might have to start reading those tabloids.

"And your beau? We looked in on you earlier tonight, he seems quite recovered!"

Somewhere above, Auntie Jadine titters. Really need to have them stop that.

"Michael George doing well," I confirm. Me and him finally have that talk he been wanting. And I answer some of his questions. Not all, but enough. For now. I'm expecting him to call me crazy, but he just nods slow. Says he always thought them Klans was jumbie, what they call haints in St. Lucia. And that his great-auntie was an Obeah woman, so he not afraid of magic. Says none of that stopping him from taking me sailing one day. I tell him I still don't make promises. But I'll think on it.

"We're delighted things are going well, Maryse," Auntie Ondine says. She looks hesitant. "Have you made a decision about the sword?"

I set down my glass, right beside the leaf-shaped blade. I ain't called it since Stone Mountain. After everything, I needed some time to just be Maryse, not nobody's champion. This sword done right by me. Yet, lie that he was, Butcher Clyde wasn't fibbing when he said I took pleasure in working out my vengeance. I think to Dr. Bisset. His emptiness. Don't want that. Nana Jean warned me accepting gifts from haints carried a price. I seen now what it's like to pay it.

But this war not over.

There's still Klans. Still Ku Kluxes. Still that damned movie. This sword carries anger paid for in the suffering of a whole people. Butcher Clyde and them couldn't have it, because it wasn't theirs to take, to twist and feed on. It been passed on to me. Mine to shape into what's needed here and now. I ain't ready to abandon that just yet. Besides, got some vengeance in me still needs working out.

I look up to see everybody quiet, waiting. Even Auntie Jadine stopped humming.

"I'm still your champion. If you'll have me."

Auntie Ondine beams and Auntie Margaret gives the barest smile, which is a lot for her. Auntie Jadine winks from above, and I wink back.

"You are indeed our champion!" Auntie Ondine pronounces.

Those words make me happier than I'd realized and I look over the sword. "You know it come to me that it ain't right this blade only binds the spirits of slave-trading chiefs and kings. What about the white folk who bought them slaves? Who worked them to death. Ain't they got penance to pay?"

Aunt Ondine gives the foxiest of grins. "Why Maryse, that's a whole *other* sword."

I almost choke on the mint julep. Another sword? A hundred questions form on my tongue. But her face turns serious.

"I'm glad you taking time to rest. But I'm afraid there's evil afoot."

I sigh, returning to my mint julep. Naturally. Always evil a-footing.

"The enemy still at they work," Auntie Margaret puts in.

"A new threat rises," Auntie Ondine goes on. She leans in. "You must go on a quest! To an isle within the Province of Rhodes!"

I stop mid-sip. "You mean Providence, Rhode Island?"

She blinks. "Isn't that what I said? The enemy has their eyes fixed there—on a man they believe can help them further infiltrate your world, open doors to worse than their Grand Cyclops. They're inculcating him with their vileness and he appears a willing vessel. He has been named their Dark Prince and—"

"Sadie's funeral in two days," I interrupt. Not sure these three understand how geography works. "Rhode Island a long ways from my bootlegging routes. But Emma has contacts in New England. We can see what they know."

"Oh," Auntie Ondine says, regretful. "Yes, that would be helpful. How is the death ritual coming along?"

"Funeral," I stress. "We call it a *funeral*. Lester organizing it. Got a big church, a choir, and everything. Uncle Will leading a Shout. Nana Jean doing the cooking. Michael

George says he might name the new inn he building after her. Don't think Macon seen the last of Sadie Watkins."

I down the mint julep, standing up. "Well, best be going."

"You still got a while yet," Auntie Ondine frets. "There's blackberry jam cake." A tempting white-frosted cake topped by blackberries up and appears. But I shake my head.

"Time don't pass here, but I need my rest. Got plans in the morning. Me and Chef gonna do something big for Sadie like she asked—something she'd like."

Auntie Ondine smiles tenderly. "She's fortunate her friends keep her memory."

"We going to a movie house—where they showing *The Birth of a Nation*."

Auntie Margaret squints over her stitching. "Mighty odd choice."

"Not staying long. Gonna clear the theater with a smoke bomb, then blow it up."

I pick up my sword, balancing it over one shoulder as I head back home, listening to Auntie Jadine cackling above, as I whistle a song of hunting Ku Kluxes in the end times.

ACKNOWLEDGMENTS

This story emerged out of a diverse visual, literary, and aural synthesis. The 1930s ex-slave narratives of the WPA. Gullah-Geechee culture. Folktales of haints and root magic. A few Beyoncé videos. Some Toni Morrison. Juke (Jook) joints. Childhood memories of reading Madeline L'Engle under the shade of a cypress. Juneteenth picnics. New Orleans Bounce. A little DJ Screw. H-town that raised me. And whispered stories of Jim Crow, the Klan, and other Southern horrors. Who says all the fantasies with

sword-wielding heroes and heroines have to be in Middle
Earth, Westeros, or even our dreams of Africa past—"copper sun or scarlet sea?"

Maybe they can happen right here, too.

Grateful to John and Alan Lomax, Zora Neale Hurston,
Lydia Parrish, and all those who worked to record and preserve the Ring Shout tradition. Praises all around to the
McIntosh County Shouters whose performances and renditions help bring those archival memories to life. Props
to Lupe Fiasco's DROGAS Wave, which served as inspiration as I tried to work this thing out. If this story had a
soundtrack, that'd be it. Appreciation also to Saidiya Hartman's Lose Your Mother, which still challenges me: "I, too,
am the afterlife of slavery."

Special thanks to fellow writer Eden Royce, who was
gracious and patient enough to walk me through Gullah
culture and language. Thanks also to my brother from
another mother Cleo Wadley Jr., who gave invaluable
recommendations to earlier drafts. You got all the inside jokes. "Nd Suth Ept." Big ups to writer, editor, and
co-creator of our own personal Black Imaginarium,
Troy L. Wiggins, for giving this story that Southern
stamp of approval. Look where we at bruh? Thanks to
the whole Tordotcom Publishing team for helping put
this together, not to mention that amazing cover design. Lastly, my greatest gratitude goes to Auntie Editor
Diana Pho. Because when I sat in a DC coffee shop pitch-

ing this story idea to you over the phone, you were the first person to say—"that sounds awesome!" Thanks for taking a chance on this, and so many other diverse and daring tales, when others might not have. Hope that airship takes you far.